"I would have preferred to hear from you."

"I thought about it," he said. "But you've done enough helping with the babies."

"I thought perhaps that you and I were about more than the babies, but maybe I was wrong," she said, looking away.

His heart slamming against his rib cage, he cupped her chin and swiveled it toward him. "You were right. You know you were."

Her eyes darkened with emotion and she stepped closer. She moved against him and slid her arms upward around his neck. She pulled his face toward hers and he couldn't remember feeling this alive. Ever.

His body was on full tilt in the arousal zone. He took a quick breath and forced himself to draw back. "I'm not sure I can pull back after this," he said. "If you're going to say no, do it now."

"Yes," she whispered. "Yes."

Dear Reader,

Have you ever been underestimated? How did you deal with it? Laugh it off? Get angry and stomp your foot? Ignore it?

All are options. For Princess Bridget Devereaux, once her life was saved by her now sister-in-law, everything changed. Now, she needs to make sure the life she's living is worth saving. What a challenge. What she doesn't know is that she is far more important than she believed.

So back to this underestimation thing.... Have you ever underestimated yourself? I think we often do. When someone comes along who believes in you, who sees you as bigger and more capable than you see yourself, it can be a hugely empowering, amazing experience.

When Princess Bridget meets Dr. Ryder McCall, he and his babies challenge her in ways she'd never dreamed. Along the way, they could end up saving each other. I hope you'll enjoy the ride to see how it all turns out....

xo,

Leanne Banks

THE DOCTOR TAKES A PRINCESS

LEANNE BANKS

Harlequin

SPECIAL EDITION

Recycling programs
for this product may
not exist in your area.

ISBN-13: 978-0-373-65609-7

THE DOCTOR TAKES A PRINCESS

Printed in U.S.A.

LEANNE BANKS

is a *New York Times* and *USA TODAY* bestselling author who is surprised every time she realizes how many books she has written. Leanne loves chocolate, the beach and new adventures. To name a few, Leanne has ridden on an elephant, stood on an ostrich egg (no, it didn't break), gone parasailing and indoor skydiving. Leanne loves writing romance because she believes in the power and magic of love. She lives in Virginia with her family and four-and-a-half-pound Pomeranian named Bijou. Visit her website at www.leannebanks.com.

This book is dedicated to all those underestimated women with tender hearts and big fears who hide it all with a big smile. Thank you for being so much more than we give you credit for.

Prologue

Ryder McCall raced the double baby stroller into the elevator just as the doors started to close. The twin boys cackled with glee at the wild ride as he pressed the button for the eighth floor. He'd already rescheduled the appointment with his attorney three times and he would have done it again if he'd known the nanny was going to bail on him. Again.

In the back of his mind, he counted his pulse. His heart rate was higher now than when he'd run a half marathon last year. His life was far different now, he thought as he glanced at the boys and caught a swishing movement behind him. Stepping to the side, he saw a woman dressed in a pink cocktail gown that skimmed over her creamy shoulders and her curvy body. The dress ended just above her knees, revealing a tempting glimpse of her legs and high-heeled sandals. The medical expert in him knew the negative impact of high heels on the human body, but the man in him was trying to remember the last time he'd been out with a woman. He was having a tough time remembering.

The woman smiled at him and gestured toward the twins. "They're adorable. I bet they keep you busy."

He nodded. "More than you could—"

The elevator suddenly jolted and dropped several feet, then stopped.

Ryder glanced at the boys at the same time he heard the woman's intake of breath. "Everyone okay?"

The twins just looked at them with wide eyes.

"Are we stuck?" the woman asked, her brow furrowed with worry.

"Let me see," he said and pushed the button for another floor. The elevator didn't move. He pushed the button to open the doors and nothing happened. He pushed the alarm button and a piercing sound filled the elevator.

The woman covered her ears. "Oh, my—"

A voice came on an intercom. "This is building security. Do you have a problem?"

"We're stuck," Ryder yelled over the terrible pulsating alarm. He heard a sob from one of the boys. A half beat later, the other started, louder.

"So sorry, sir. We'll come and fix it soon."

"Soon," he echoed as the twins began to cry in earnest. "When is soon?"

"As soon as possible," the woman on the intercom said and there was a clicking noise. The alarm shut off, but the boys were in high gear.

"Oh, the poor things. They must be frightened," the woman in the elevator said. She paused a moment, then shrugged. "Here, I'll hold one of them."

Ryder shot a skeptical glance at her. "They haven't had their baths and they're very messy eaters." Tyler was wearing a gross combination of yellow and orange on his blue shirt while Travis clearly had not enjoyed his strained peas. Green smudges decorated the light blue shirt that matched his brother's.

The woman made a tsking sound. "Well, we have to do something. We can't let them keep screaming." She set her purse on the floor and held out her hands. "Go ahead, give one of them to me," she insisted in a voice that sounded as if she were accustomed to having her orders followed.

As a medical doctor and acting chief adviser for the residents at Texas Medical Center, he, too, was accustomed to having his orders followed. This time, though, he decided to allow the woman to take Tyler because the baby was clearly beyond upset. As soon as he set the boy in her arms, she bobbed as if she'd handled a crying baby before. Ryder hauled Travis out of his stroller seat and also bobbed.

The woman made soothing sounds and Tyler gradually quieted between hiccups. As usual, Travis took a little longer. He was the louder boy of the two.

"That's better," she said. "Who am I holding?"

"Tyler," Ryder said. "This is Travis. I'm Ryder Mc-Call. Thank you for your help."

"You're quite welcome," she said in a voice that seemed to combine several accents, none of which originated from Texas. "I'm Bridget," she said and fanned herself with the shawl draped over her arm. "Whew, it's getting warm already."

"And it's only going to get hotter until they fix the elevator. Are you feeling faint?" he asked, aware that plenty of people would grow light-headed in this situation.

She shook her head. "No."

"I'd offer you some water, but I was in a hurry when I left the house, so all I've got are bottles for the boys."

"Well, at least you have that," she said and glanced at her watch. "I hope we're not stuck for long. Perhaps I should call my friends." She bent toward the floor and shook her head. "I'm sorry, Tyler. I'm going to have to put you down for a moment," she murmured and carefully placed the tot in his stroller seat. She picked up her phone and punched some numbers, then frowned.

"Let me guess," Ryder said. "No service."

She nodded.

"Figures. The steel doors can sustain most catastrophes known to man, so they're bound to make it difficult to get a cell connection."

She bit her lip and winced. "Oh, I wonder if someone will call my security."

"They're on their way," he said, wondering if she hadn't understood the conversation he'd had with the woman earlier. Maybe she hadn't heard correctly, he thought, between the alarm bleeping and the boys screaming. "At least, they better be on their way. I hope the boys don't—"

"Need a diaper change?" she asked, nodding in understanding. "Time for the—"

"Nanny," he said in complete agreement. "I just wish I could find one who would stay around longer than two weeks."

"That sounds difficult. Are you working with an agency?"

He nodded. "Part of the problem is I work long hours."

"Hmm, and your wife?"

"I don't have a wife," he said.

Her eyes widened. "Oh, that must make it very difficult."

Ryder sighed. "I'm actually the boys' godfather. My brother and his wife were killed in an automobile accident one month ago."

Bridget gasped. "That's terrible. Those poor boys, and you, oh my goodness. Do you have any help at all?"

"Not unless I hire them," he muttered. "Do you have any children?"

She shook her head quickly, the same way he would have before he'd learned he would be raising the boys. "Two baby nieces," she said.

"That's how you knew to bob up and down with Tyler," he said.

"Yes," Bridget said and glanced at her watch again, growing uneasy. She'd agreed to the charity appearance she would be attending as a favor to her sister's long-time friend, and her security was only a three-button code away if she should need them. If her sister's friend became uneasy, however, she might call Valentina.

Valentina might call security to check on her and...
She shuddered at the public scene that would cause.
Bridget was here in Dallas to do the job her brother had
asked of her and as soon as she was done, she was off
to Italy.

It was so warm that she was getting past the glow
stage. Right now, she probably looked like she'd just finished a spinning class, although she did those as rarely
as possible. Getting sweaty wouldn't matter that much
to her if she weren't being photographed. During the last
year and a half, however, it had been drilled into her that
her appearance in front of the camera was a reflection
of her country. It was her duty to look immaculate and
to avoid scandal at all cost.

Bridget had slipped a few times on both counts. She
might be a princess, but she wasn't perfect. Nor was
she particularly patient. She could tell that Ryder, the
other adult in the elevator, wasn't patient either. He was
glancing upward as if he were assessing the structure
of the lift.

"You're not thinking of climbing out, are you?" she
couldn't resist asking.

"If no one shows up, I may have to," he said.

"And what were you planning to do with the babies?"
she demanded, panicked at the prospect of being left
alone with the twins. Now that she thought of it, Ryder's
presence had made her feel much more reassured.

He shot her a level look. "The purpose of getting out
would be to ensure safety for all of us."

He looked like a no-nonsense kind of man, strong,
perhaps intolerant of anyone weaker than himself.

Which would include her. Okay, she was making assumptions. But what else could she bloody do? She was stuck in an elevator with the man. She couldn't deny the appeal of his strong jaw and lean but muscular body. She also couldn't deny her admiration that he had taken on his brother's orphaned twins.

An instant parent of twin boys? The mere thought made her sweat even more. Bridget would have forced herself to accept her responsibility in such a situation, but hopefully with sufficient support. Multiple children, multiple nannies.

She sighed, glancing at the emergency button. "We've heard nothing. Do you think we should call again?"

"It will make the boys cry again," he said, clearly torn.

"I'll take Tyler," she said and picked up the baby. He flashed her a smile that gave her a burst of pleasure despite their situation. "You're a little flirt, aren't you?" she said and tickled his chin.

Ryder stabbed the button and the shrieking alarm started. Tyler's smile immediately fell and his eyes filled with fear. He began to scream. His brother began to wail.

Seconds later, the alarm stopped and a voice came on the intercom, but Bridget couldn't make out the conversation with Ryder as she tried to comfort Tyler. The only thing she knew was that Ryder had spoken in a firm, commanding voice that rivaled that of her brother's, and anyone in their right mind had better obey.

The intercom voice went away, but the babies still cried. Bridget and Tyler bobbed. "What did they say?"

"They said they would take care of us in five minutes," he yelled over the cries of the boys.

"How did you do that?"

"I told them I was climbing out in three," he said.

"Effective. I wonder if I should try that sometime," she mused. "Is there anything else we can do to settle them down?" she asked loudly, still shielding Tyler's closest ear with her hand.

A long-suffering expression crossed his face. "Just one thing," he said. "Row, row, row your boat, gently down the stream."

Bridget stared in amazement at this man who reminded her of a modern-day warrior singing a children's song and something inside her shifted. The sensation made her feel light-headed. Alarm shot through her. Or perhaps, it was the heat. Pushing the odd feeling and any self-consciousness aside, she sang along.

Six minutes later, the elevator doors opened with a swarm of firemen, paramedics and Bridget's security guard standing outside.

"Your Highness," her security guard said, extending his hand to her.

"Just a second," she said, putting Tyler into his stroller seat.

"Your Highness?" Ryder echoed, studying her with a curious gaze. "Why didn't you—"

"It—it causes a fuss," she said. "Will you be okay? Will the children be okay?"

"We're fine," he said, and she felt foolish for questioning such a capable man.

"Well, thank you," she said and extended her hand

to his, noting that his hands were smooth, but large and strong. She felt an odd little spark and immediately pulled back. "And good luck."

"Your Highness, a medical professional is waiting to examine you," her security said as she stepped off the lift.

"I don't need a medical professional," she murmured. "I need a cosmetic miracle."

Chapter One

Sitting at the kitchen table of her brother-in-law's ranch, Bridget watched Zach Logan hug her sister Valentina as if he were leaving for a yearlong journey. Instead, she knew he would be gone for only a couple of nights. Bridget resisted the urge to roll her eyes. Zach and Valentina just seemed so gooey in love.

"Call me if you need anything," he told her, then swung his young daughter, Katiana, up into his arms. "Are you going to be good for your mommy?"

Katiana solemnly nodded.

"Give me a kiss," he said.

The toddler kissed his cheek and wrapped her little arms around his neck.

Despite her earlier reaction, the scene tugged at Bridget's heart. She knew Zach and Tina had gone through some tough times before they'd gotten married.

Zach shot Bridget a firm glance that instinctively

made her sit up straighter. He was that kind of man, confident with a strong will. Although she was happy Tina had found happiness with him, Bridget knew she would want a totally different kind of man. Charming, average intelligence, playful and most likely Italian.

"You," he said, pointing his finger at Bridget. "Stay out of elevators."

She laughed. "I can only promise that for a few days. When I go back to Dallas, I'm sure I'll have to face more elevators if I'm going to complete Stefan's latest job for me. If I have anything to do with it, I'm going to take care of it as quickly as possible."

Tina shot her a sideways glance. "Are you saying you're already tired of us?"

Bridget shook her head and walked to give her sister a hug. "Of course I'm not tired of you. But you know I've had a dream of having a long-delayed gap year in Italy and studying art for years now. I want to make that dream come true while I'm still young."

Tina made a scoffing sound, but still returned the hug. "You're far from losing your youth, but I agree you deserve a break. You've taken on the bulk of public appearances since I left Chantaine and moved here. I don't understand why you didn't take a break before coming here. I'm sure Stefan would have let you."

Stefan, their brother, the crown prince, could be the most demanding person on the planet, but what Tina said was true. He not only would have allowed Bridget a break, he had also encouraged it. "I want a year. A whole year. And he believes Chantaine needs more doctors. I agree. Especially after what happened to Eve—"

Her voice broke, taking her by surprise. She'd thought she'd gotten her feelings under control.

Tina patted her back with sympathy. "You still feel guilty about that. I know Eve wishes you didn't."

Bridget took a careful breath, reining in her emotions. "She saved my life when the crowd was going to stampede me. Pushed me aside and threw herself in front of me. I'm just so glad she survived it and recovered. I don't know what I would do if she hadn't…" Her throat closed up again.

"Well, she survived and you did, too. That's what's important," Zach said and pulled Bridget into a brotherly hug. "And now that you're in my territory, I want you to think twice before getting on elevators."

Tina laughed. "So protective," she said. "It's a wonder he doesn't find some kind of testing device for you to use so you won't get stuck again."

Zach rubbed his chin thoughtfully. "Not a bad idea. Maybe—"

"Forget it," Bridget said, the knot in her chest easing at the love she felt from both her sister and her brother-in-law. "I'll be fine. Think about it. How many people do you know who have gotten stuck in elevators? Especially more than once?"

"You were a good soldier," Tina said in approval. "And you still showed up for your appearance at Keely's charity event."

"She probably wasn't expecting me in my sad state with droopy hair and a dress with baby-food stain on it."

"Oh, she said they loved you. Found you charming.

Were delighted by your story about the elevator. Most important, the donations increased after your arrival."

"Well, I guess baby-food stains are good for something, then. I'll leave you two lovebirds to finish your goodbyes in private. Safe travels, Zach."

"You bet," he said.

Bridget scooped up her cup of hot tea and walked upstairs to the guest room where she was staying. Her sister had redecorated the room in soothing shades of green and blue. The ranch should have given Bridget a sense of serenity. After all, she was miles from Stefan and his to-do list for her. She was away from Chantaine where she was recognized and haunted by the paparazzi whenever she left the palace. But Bridget never seemed to be able to escape the restlessness inside her. That was why she'd decided to skip a short vacation and take care of this significant task Stefan had asked of her. After that, she could take her trip to Italy and find her peace again.

No one had ever accused Bridget of being deep. She voiced her distress and upset to her family at will, but presented the rest of the world with a cheery effervescent face. It was her job.

Some of the conditions she'd witnessed during the past year and a half, the sights and sounds of children sick in the hospital, Chantaine's citizens struggling with poverty, cut her to the quick and it had been difficult to keep her winsome attitude intact. It irritated her how much she now had to struggle to maintain a superficial air. Life had been so much easier when she hadn't faced others in need. Life had been easier when someone hadn't been willing to sacrifice her life for the sake of Bridget's safety.

Even though Eve had indeed survived and thrived since the accident, something inside Bridget had changed. And she wasn't sure she liked it. Eve and Stefan had fallen in love and married. Eve cared for Stefan's out-of-wedlock daughter as if she were her own. On the face of it, everything was wonderful.

Deep down, though, Bridget wondered if her life was really worth saving. What had she done that made her worthy of such an act?

She squeezed her eyes shut and swore under her breath. "Stop asking that question," she whispered harshly to herself.

Steeling herself against the ugly swarm of emotions, Bridget set her cup of tea on the table. She would complete the task Stefan asked of her. Then maybe she would have settled the score inside her, the score she couldn't quite explain even to herself. Afterward she would go to Italy and hopefully she would find the joy and lightness she'd lost.

After three days of being unable to meet with the head of residents at Texas Medical Center of Dallas, Bridget seethed with impatience. Dr. Gordon Walters was never available, and all her calls to his office went unanswered. Thank goodness for connections. Apparently Tina's friend Keely knew a doctor at University Hospital and there just happened to be a meet and greet for interns, doctors and important donors at a hotel near the hospital on Tuesday night.

Bridget checked into the hotel and her security took the room next to hers. One advantage of being at Zach's ranch meant security was superfluous. Not so in Dallas. She dressed carefully because she needed to impress and to be taken seriously. A black dress with heels. She resisted the urge to paint her lips red. The old Bridget wouldn't have batted an eye.

Frowning into the bathroom mirror in her suite, she wondered what that meant. Well, hell, if Madonna could wear red lipstick and be taken seriously, why couldn't she? She smoothed her fingers over her head and tucked one side of her hair behind her left ear. She'd colored her hair darker lately. It fit her mood.

She frowned again into the mirror. Maybe she would dye it blond when she moved to Italy.

She punched the code for her security on her cell phone. Raoul picked up immediately. "Yes, Your Highness."

"I'm ready. Please stay in the background," she said.

"Yes, ma'am. But I shall join you on the elevator."

A couple moments later, she rode said elevator to the floor which held the meeting rooms and ballrooms. A host stood outside the ballroom which housed the cocktail party she would attend. "Name?" he asked as she approached him.

She blinked, unaccustomed to being screened. Doors opened at the mention of her title. Not in Texas, she supposed. "Bridget Devereaux and escort," she said, because Raoul was beside her.

The man flipped through several pages and checked off her name. "Welcome," he said. "Please go in."

"The nerve of the man," Raoul said as they entered the ballroom full of people. "To question a member of the royal family," he fumed as he surveyed the room.

Bridget smiled. "Novel experience," she said. "I'm looking for Dr. Gordon Walters. If you see him, by all means, please do tell me."

Thirty minutes later, Bridget was ready to pull out her hair. Every time she mentioned Dr. Walters's name, people clammed up. She couldn't squeeze even a bit of information about the man from anyone.

Frustrated, she accepted a glass of wine and decided to take another tack.

Dr. Ryder McCall checked his watch for the hundredth time in ten minutes. How much longer did he need to stay? The latest nanny he'd hired had seemed okay when he'd left tonight, but after his previous experiences, he couldn't be sure. He caught a glimpse of the back of a woman with dark brown wavy hair and paused. Something about her looked familiar.

The dress was classic and on a woman with a different body, it would have evoked images of that actress. What was her name? Audrey something. But this woman had curves which evoked entirely different thoughts. The sight of the woman's round derriere reminded Ryder of the fact that he hadn't been with a woman in a while. Too long, he thought and adjusted his tie.

Curious, he moved so that he could catch a side view of her. Oh yeah, he thought, his gaze sliding over her feminine form from her calves to her thighs to the thrust of her breasts. He could easily imagine her minus the dress. His body responded. Then he glanced upward to her face and recognition slammed into him.

The woman speaking so animatedly to one of his

top residents, Timothy Bing, was the same woman he'd met in the elevator the other night. Princess whatever. Bridget, he recalled. And of course, his top resident was utterly enthralled. Why wouldn't he be? The poor resident was sleep-deprived, food-deprived and sex-deprived.

Ryder was suffering from the same deprivation albeit for different reasons. He wondered why she was here tonight. Might as well cure his curiosity, he thought, if he couldn't cure his other deprivations. He walked toward the two of them.

Timothy only had eyes for Her Highness. Ryder cleared his throat. Both Timothy and the woman turned to look at him.

Timothy stiffened as if he were a marine and he'd just glimpsed a superior. Ryder almost wondered if he would salute. "Dr. McCall," he said.

Bridget looked at him curiously. "Doctor?" she echoed. "I didn't know you were a doctor."

"We didn't have much time to discuss our occupations. Your Highness," he added.

Out of the corner of his vision, he saw Timothy's eyes bulge in surprise. "Highness," he said. "Are you a queen or something? I thought you said you were a representative of Chantaine."

Bridget shot Ryder a glare, then smiled sweetly at Timothy. "I am a representative of Chantaine. A royal representative, and I hope you'll consider the proposal I gave you about serving in Chantaine for a couple of years in exchange for a scholarship and all your living expenses."

Ryder stared at the woman in horrified silence. She

was trying to seduce away one of his prized residents. Timothy was brilliant. His next step should be to one of the top neurological hospitals in the States.

Ryder laughed. "Not in a million years," he said.

Bridget furrowed her brow. "Why not? It's a generous offer. Dr. Bing would benefit, as would Chantaine."

"Because Dr. Bing is not going to make a gigantic misstep in his career by taking off for an island retreat when he could be one of the top neurological surgeons in America."

Bridget's furrow turned to a frown. "I find it insulting that you consider a temporary move to Chantaine a misstep. Our citizens suffer from neurological illnesses, too. Is it not the goal of a doctor to heal? Why should there be a prejudice against us just because we reside in a beautiful place? Does that mean we shouldn't have treatment?"

"I wasn't suggesting that your country doesn't deserve medical care. It's my job, however, to advise Dr. Bing to make the best decisions in advancing his career and knowledge."

Princess Bridget crossed her arms over her chest and looked down her nose at him. "I thought that was Dr. Gordon Walters's job, although the man is nowhere to be found."

Timothy made a choking sound. "Excuse me," he said. "I need to…" He walked quickly away without finishing his sentence.

"Well, now you've done it," she said. "I was having a perfectly lovely conversation with Dr. Bing and you ruined it."

"Me?"

"Yes, you. The whole tenor of our conversation changed when you appeared. Dr. Bing was actually open to considering my offer to come to Chantaine."

"Dr. Bing wanted to get into your pants," Ryder said and immediately regretted his blunt statement.

Bridget shot him a shocked glance. "You're the most insulting man I've ever met."

"You clearly haven't met many residents," he said wearily. "I apologize if I offended you, but Timothy Bing doesn't belong in Chantley or wherever you said you're from."

"Chantaine," she said between gritted teeth. "I will accept your apology if you can direct me to Dr. Gordon Walters. He is the man I must meet."

Ryder sighed. "I'm afraid I'm going to have to disappoint you. Dr. Gordon Walters is not here tonight. He hasn't been working in the position as chief resident adviser for some time. It's not likely he'll return."

She cocked her head to one side and frowned further. "Then who will take his place?"

"No one will take his place. Dr. Walters is rightfully loved and respected. I am serving as his temporary successor."

Realization crossed her face. "How wonderful," she said, when she clearly found the news anything but.

Bloody hell, Bridget thought, clenching her fingers together. Now she'd put herself in a mess. She took a deep breath and tried to calm herself. Yes, she and Dr. McCall had engaged in a spirited discussion, but surely he would come around once he heard more about Chantaine and the program she was offering.

"Well, I'm glad I've finally found the person who is currently in charge. Our first meeting in the elevator showed that you and I are both responsible, reasonable adults. I'm sure we'll be able to come to an understanding on this matter," she said, imbuing her words with every bit of positive energy she could muster.

Dr. McCall shot her a skeptical glance. "I'll agree with your first point, but I can't promise anything on the second. It's good to see you again, Your Highness." His gaze gave her a quick sweep from head to toe and back again. "Nice dress. Good evening," he said and turned to leave.

It took Bridget an extra second to recover from the understated compliment that inexplicably flustered before she went after him. "Wait, please," she said.

Dr. McCall stopped and turned, looking at her with a raised eyebrow. "Yes?"

"I really do need to discuss Chantaine's medical needs with you. I'm hoping we can come to some sort of agreement."

"I already told you I couldn't recommend that Timothy Bing spend two years in your country," he said.

"But you have other students," she said. "I'm sure you have students interested in many different areas of medical care. Coming to Chantaine would enable the physicians to get hands-on experience. Plus there's the matter of the financial assistance we would offer."

"I'm sorry, Your High—"

"Oh, please," she said, unable to contain her impatience. "Call me Bridget. We've sung together in an elevator, for bloody sake."

His lips twitched slightly. "True. Bridget, I'm not

sure I can help you. Again, my number-one priority is guiding my students to make the best career decisions."

Her heart sank. "Well, the least you can do is give me an opportunity to discuss Chantaine's needs and what we have to offer."

He sighed and shrugged his shoulders in a discouraging way, then pulled a card from his pocket. "Okay. Here's my card. My schedule is very busy, but call my assistant and she'll work you in."

Work her in. Bridget clenched her teeth slightly at the words, but forced a smile. "Thank you. You won't regret it."

"Hmm," he said in a noncommittal tone and walked away.

She barely resisted the urge to stick out her tongue at him.

Raoul appeared by her side. "Are you all right, Your Highness? You look upset."

"I do?" she asked, composing herself into what she hoped look like a serene expression. She was finding it more and more difficult to pull off instant serenity these days. "I'm fine," she said. "I've just encountered a slight obstacle to completing my assignment for Chantaine."

She watched Ryder McCall's broad shoulders and tall form as he wove through the crowd. Slight obstacle was putting it mildly, but she'd learned that a positive attitude could get a woman through a lot of tricky spots. "I need to know everything about Dr. Ryder McCall by morning, if not before," she muttered and glanced around the room. It was amazing what one could learn about a person in a social situation such as this. She might as well make the best of it.

* * *

Ryder walked into his house braced for chaos. His home life had become one big state of chaos bigger than the state of Texas since he'd inherited his brother's boys. Instead of pandemonium, his home was dark and quiet, except for the sound of a baseball game. Ryder spotted his longtime pal Marshall lounging on the leather couch with a box of half-eaten pizza on the coffee table and a beer in his hand.

"Your sitter called me," Marshall said, not rising. "As your official backup. She said one of her kids got sick, so she couldn't stay. Just curious, where am I on that backup list?"

Pretty far down, Ryder thought, but didn't admit it. There were two middle-aged neighbors, an aunt on the other side of town and his admin assistant before Marshall. Ryder suspected he'd called in favors too often if everyone had refused but Marshall. "Thanks for coming. How are the boys?"

Marshall cracked a wily grin. "Great. Gave them a few Cheerios, wore them out and tossed them into bed."

"Bath?" he asked.

"The sitter took care of that before I got here. That Travis is a pistol. Didn't want to go to sleep, so I gave him my best Garth Brooks."

Ryder gave a tired smile. "Must have worked. I'll give a quick check and be right back."

"Cold one's waiting," Marshall said.

Ryder trusted Marshall to a degree, but he didn't think leaving the kids with his buddy from high school on a regular basis was a good idea. He wouldn't put it past Marshall to slip the boys a sip from his beer if he was desperate enough. When pressured, Marshall could get a little too creative, like the time he hot-wired the car of one of the school's top wrestlers because his own car had died.

Marshall owned a chain of auto-mechanic shops across Texas. He wore his hair in a ponytail and tattoos were stamped over his arms and back. He hadn't attended college, but he'd made a success of himself. Most people couldn't understand their friendship because they appeared to be total opposites, but a mutual appreciation for baseball, some shared holiday dinners which had always included hotdogs and hamburgers and the fact that they both tried to show up during the hard times had made them like family.

With his brother Cory gone, Marshall was the closest thing to family Ryder had. His gut twisted at the thought, but he shoved the feeling aside and gently opened the door to the nursery. He'd learned to walk with stealthlike quiet during the last month. The possibility of waking the boys made him break into a cold sweat.

Moving toward the closest crib, he glanced inside and even in the dark, he knew that this was Tyler, and he was in Travis's bed. Travis was in Tyler's bed. He wasn't going to complain. They were both lying on their backs in la-la land. Which was exactly where he would like to be.

Instead, he walked on quiet footsteps out of the room and gently closed the door behind him. Returning to the den, he saw Marshall still sprawled on his sofa with the same beer in his hand.

"They're asleep," Ryder said and sank into a leather chair next to the sofa. He raked his hand through his hair.

"I coulda told you that," Marshall said. "I made sure they would sleep well tonight."

He shot a quick glance at Marshall. "You didn't give them any booze, did you?"

Marshall looked offended. "Booze to babies? What kind of nut job do you think I am?"

"Well, you aren't around kids very much," Ryder said.

"Maybe not now, but I was an in-demand babysitter in junior high school. Some things you don't forget. And just in case you're worried, this is my second beer. I wouldn't go on a bender when I was taking care of your kids."

Chagrined, Ryder rubbed his chin. "You got me. Sorry, bud. Being in charge of two kids is making me a little crazy."

"A little?" Marshall said and shook his head. "You've turned into the nut job. You know what your problem is, you're no fun anymore. Those babies sense it and it gets them all uptight, too. It's like a virus. You spread it to the babysitters and it makes them crazy, so they quit. You need to get laid and go to a ball game."

"Thanks for the advice," Ryder said. "I'll take your advice in a decade or so."

"Lord help us if you wait that long," Marshall said. "Maybe I could set you up with somebody. Take the edge off."

Ryder slid him a sideways glance. "I'll pass. You and

I may root for the Texas Rangers, but we don't share the same taste in women."

"Your loss," Marshall said, sitting upright. "I know some women who could wear you out and make you sleep like a baby."

"I've learned babies don't always sleep that well."

"It's your aura," Marshall said. "That's what Jenny, my ex, would say. Your aura is poisoning your environment."

"A dependable nanny is what I need," Ryder said.

"Well, if you can get a sitter, I've got tickets to the Rangers game on Thursday. Take care, buddy," he said, rising from the couch and patting Ryder on the shoulder. "Keep the faith, bud. And move me up on that backup list. I'm more dependable than your Aunt Joanie. I bet she's always busy."

Ryder smiled despite himself. "You got it. Thanks. If I can find a sitter, I'll go to that game with you."

"I'll believe it when I see it. 'Night," Marshall said and loped out of the house.

Ryder sank farther into his chair, kicked off his shoes and propped his shoes onto the coffee table. He considered reaching for that beer, but drinking anything would require too much energy. Hearing the roar of the crowd and the occasional crack of the bat hitting the ball from the game on his flat-screen TV with surround system, he closed his eyes.

Making sure the twins were safe, taking care of his patients and covering for Dr. Walters were the most important things in his life, but he knew he needed help, especially with the twins. He'd never dreamed how difficult it would be to find dependable caretakers for the boys. His head began to pound. He could feel his blood pressure rising. Pinching the bridge of his nose, for one moment, he deliberately chose *not* to think about the next nanny he would need to hire and the deteriorating mental health of his mentor, Dr. Walters.

Ryder thought back to his high school days when he'd been catcher and Marshall had pitched. They'd won the state championship senior year. That weekend had been full of celebration. He remembered a cheerleader who had paid attention to him for the first time. She'd given him a night full of memories. Blonde, curvy and wiggly, she'd kept him busy. He hadn't lasted long the first time, but he'd done better the second and the third.

His lips tilted upward at the memory. He remembered the thrill of winning. There had never been a happier moment in his life. He sighed, and the visual of a different woman filled his mind. She had dark shoulder-length hair with a wicked red mouth and cool blue eyes. She wore a black dress that handled her curves the same way a man would. She would be a seductive combination of soft and firm with full breasts and inviting hips. She would kiss him into insanity and make him want more. He would slide his hands into her feminine wetness and make her gasp, then make her gasp again when he thrust inside her....

Ryder blinked. He was brick-hard and his heart was racing as if he were having sex. He swore out loud.

He couldn't believe himself. Maybe Marshall was right. Maybe he just really needed to get laid. His only problem was that the woman in his daydream had been

Problem Princess Bridget Devereaux. Yep, Marshall was right. Ryder was a nut job.

Bridget read Dr. Ryder McCall's dossier for the hundredth time in three days. He hadn't had the easiest upbringing in the world. His father had died when he was eight years old. His mother had died two years ago.

Ryder had played baseball in high school and won an academic scholarship. He'd graduated first in his college class, then first in his medical-school class.

His older brother, Cory, had played football and earned a college scholarship. Unfortunately, he was injured, so he dropped out, took a job as a department-store manager and married his high-school sweetheart. They'd waited to have children. Six months after the birth of twin boys, they'd attended an anniversary dinner but never made it home. A tractor trailer jackknifed in front of them on the freeway. They both died before they arrived at the emergency room.

An unbelievable tragedy. Even though Bridget had lost both her parents within years of each other, she had never been close to them. Ryder had clearly been close to his brother. Now, a man who had previously been unswervingly focused on his studies and career, was alone with those precious motherless babies.

Her heart broke every time she read his story. This was one of those times she wished she had a magic wand that would solve all of Ryder's problems and heal his pain. But she didn't. As much as she wished it were true, Bridget was all too certain of her humanity.

In the midst of all of this, she still had a job to do. She needed to bring doctors to Chantaine, and Dr. McCall's assistant hedged every time Bridget attempted to make an appointment. She would give the assistant two more tries, then Bridget would face Ryder in his own territory. If he thought an assistant would keep her at bay, he had no concept of her will. Surprise, surprise, especially to herself. She may have portrayed an airy, charming personality, but underneath it all, she was growing a backbone.

Chapter Two

Ryder left the hospital and picked up the boys after the latest sitter unexpectedly informed him that her child had a medical appointment she could not skip. He had an important meeting with several members of the hospital board this afternoon which *he* could not skip. He hated to press his admin assistant into baby service again, but it couldn't be helped.

After wrestling the boys in and out of car seats and the twin stroller, he felt like he'd run a 10K race as he pushed the stroller into his office suite. Instantly noting that his admin assistant was absent from her desk, he felt his stomach twist with dread. She'd left her desk tidy and organized as usual. She'd also left a note on his desk. He snatched it up and read it.

Miss Bridget Devereaux called 3x this a.m. I can't put her off forever. Gone to my anniversary celebration as discussed. Thank you for letting me off.

—Maryann

Ryder swore out loud then remembered the boys were in the room with him. "Don't ever say that word," he told them. "Bad word."

He recalled Maryann asking for the afternoon off—it had to have been a week or so ago. He'd been busy when she asked and hadn't given it a second thought. Now, he had to juggle his boys and an important meeting. He shook his head. Women managed children and careers all the time. Why was it so difficult for him? He was a healthy, intelligent man. He'd run marathons, worked more than twenty-four hours straight, brought a man back to life in the E.R., but taking care of these boys made him feel like a train wreck.

Ryder sat down at his desk and flipped through his contact list on his computer for someone he could call to watch the boys during his meeting. He sent a few emails and made three calls. All he got were voice mails.

"Well, hello, Phantom Man," a feminine voice called from the doorway.

Ryder swallowed an oath. Just what he needed right now. He didn't even need to look to know it was *Princess Persistent*. But he did and couldn't deny that she was a sight for sore eyes. Wearing another black dress, although this one looked a slight bit more like business wear, she smiled at him with that wicked red mouth that reminded him of what he hadn't had in a long time.

Dismissing the thought, he lifted his hand. "I have no time to talk. Important meeting in less than—" He glanced at the clock. "Thirty minutes. Got to find someone one to watch the boys."

"Not having any luck?" she asked.

"No."

"You sound desperate," she said, sympathy lacking in her tone.

"Not desperate," he said. "Pressed."

"Oh, well as soon as you give me a time for our meeting, I'll get out of your way."

"I already told you I don't have time," he said in a voice that no one in their right mind would question.

She shrugged. "All I want is for you to pull up your calendar and ink me in," she said. "You already agreed."

"Not—"

She crossed her arms over her chest. "You have your job. I have mine."

Travis arched against the stroller restraints as if he wanted out. The baby wore an expression of displeasure, which would soon turn to defiance and fury, which would also include unpleasant sound effects. Ryder loosened the strap and pulled him into his arms.

Tyler looked up expectantly and began the same arching action against the stroller. Ryder withheld an oath.

"Want some help?" Bridget asked.

"Yes," he said. "If you could hold Tyler, I have one more person I can—" He stopped as he watched her settle the baby on her hip. An idea sprang to mind. "Can you keep them for an hour or so?"

Her eyes widened in alarm. "An hour?" she echoed. "Or so?"

"Just for this meeting," he said. "I'll leave as soon as possible."

She shot him a considering look. "In exchange for an opportunity to discuss Chantaine's medical proposition with you, and you having an *open mind.*"

"I agree to the first half. The second is going to be tough."

"How tough would it be to take your twins to your important meeting?" she challenged.

The woman was playing dirty. "Okay," he said. "As long as you understand, my first priority is my residents' professional success."

"Done," she said. "Did you bring a blanket and some food?"

"Whatever the sitter keeps in the diaper bag," he said, relief flowing through him like a cool stream of water. "Thank you," he said, setting Travis in the stroller seat. "I'll see you after the meeting," he said and closed the office door behind him.

Bridget stared at the babies and they stared at her. Travis began to wiggle and make a frown face.

"Now, don't you start," she said, pointing her finger at him. "You haven't even given me a chance." She set Tyler in the other stroller seat and dove into the diaper bag and struck gold. "A blanket," she said. "You're going to love this," she said and spread it on the floor. Afterward, she set Travis on the blanket, followed by Tyler.

The boys looked at her expectantly.

"What?" she asked. "You're free from the bondage of the stroller. Enjoy yourselves." She narrowed her eyes. "Just don't start crawling or anything. Okay? Let's see what else is in the bag."

Unfortunately, not much. She used up the small

container of Cheerios within the first fifteen minutes and fifteen minutes after that, both boys had lost interest in the small set of blocks. She pulled out a musical toy and helped them work that over for several minutes.

Peekaboo killed a few more minutes, but then Bridget started to feel a little panicky. She needed more snacks and toys if she was going to keep the little darlings entertained. Grabbing some blank paper from Ryder's desk, she gave each boy a sheet.

Travis immediately put it in his mouth.

"Let's try something else," she said and crumpled the paper.

He smiled as if he liked the idea. Great, she thought. More paper. She crumpled a few sheets into a ball and tossed it at them. They loved that. They threw paper all over the room.

After a few more minutes, Travis began to fuss, stuffing his fist in his mouth.

"Hungry?" It would help so much if they could tell her what they needed. Luckily two bottles were also stuffed in the bag. She pulled out one and began to feed Travis. Tyler's face crumpled and he began to cry.

"Great, great," she muttered and awkwardly situated both boys on her lap as she fed them both their bottles.

They drained them in no time. Travis burped on her dress.

Bridget grimaced. A second later, Tyler gave her the same favor.

At least they weren't crying, she thought, but then she sniffed, noticing an unpleasant odor. A quick check revealed Travis had left a deposit in his diaper.

* * *

Ryder opened the door to his office prepared for screaming, crying, accusations from Bridget. Instead the boys were sprawled across her lap while she sang a medical magazine to the tune of *Frère Jacques*. He had to admit it was pretty inventive. His office looked like a disaster zone with papers strewn everywhere and he smelled the familiar, distinct scent of dirty diapers. He must have wrinkled his nose.

She did the same. "I didn't think it would be considerate to toss the diapers into the hallway, so they're in the trash can. I bundled them up as best as I could."

The boys looked safe and content. That was what was important. "It looks like you had a good time."

"Not bad," she said with a smile. "Considering my resources. You're really not set up for babies here."

"I can't agree more," he said and snatched up a few wads of paper. "What were you doing?"

"Playing ball with paper. It worked until Travis was determined to eat it." She gingerly lifted one of the boys in Ryder's direction. "So, when do we have our discussion?"

He tucked Tyler into the stroller and followed with Travis. Ryder was tempted to name a time next year but knew that wouldn't be fair. Better to get it over with. "Tonight, at my house," he said. "Do you like Chinese?"

"I prefer Italian or Mediterranean," she said, frowning as she rose to her feet. "At your house?"

"It's the one and only time I can guarantee for the foreseeable future."

She sighed. "It's not what I hoped for. How am I going to have your undivided attention?"

"Maybe we'll get lucky and they'll go to sleep," he said.

Four hours later, Bridget could barely remember what she'd said or eaten for dinner. The boys had taken a nap in the car on the way home and woken up cranky. She suspected they hadn't gotten enough of an afternoon nap. Although she resented the fact that she wasn't getting Ryder's undivided attention during their discussion, she couldn't really blame him. In fact, despite the fact that he was clearly a strong man, she could tell that caring for the twins was wearing on him. He loved them and would protect them with his life, but the man needed consistent help.

It was close to eleven before the twins truly settled down.

"I'd offer you a ride to wherever you're staying, but I can't pull the boys out of bed again," he said, after he had made the trip up and down the stairs five times.

His eyes filled with weariness, he raked a hand through his hair. Her heart tugged at his quandary. The urge to help, to fix, was overwhelming. "My security is always close by. He can collect me. It's no problem."

"I keep forgetting you're a princess," he said.

"Maybe it's the baby formula on my dress," she said drily.

"Maybe," he said, meeting her gaze. The moment swelled between them.

Bridget felt her chest grow tight and took a breath to alleviate the sensation.

"I'm sure you're tired. You could stay here if you want," he offered. "I have a guest room and bath."

Bridget blinked. She *was* tired, but staying here? "I don't have a change of clothes."

He shrugged. "I can give you a shirt to sleep in."

The prospect of sleeping in Ryder's shirt was wickedly seductive. Plus, she *was* tired. "I'd like to get your nanny situation in order for you."

"That would be a dream come true," he said. "Everything I've done so far hasn't worked."

"There may be a fee for an agency," she said. "I'm not sure how it works here. I'll have to ask my sister."

"I took the first and second suggestions that were given to me and they didn't pan out. It's imperative that I have excellent care for the boys. "

"I can see that," she said. "But do you also realize that you will have to make some adjustments as time goes on? Later, there will be sports and school activities where parents are expected to attend." Bridget remembered that neither of her parents had attended her school activities. Occasionally a nanny had shown up, but never her parents. "Have you figured out how you'll address that?"

He frowned thoughtfully. "I haven't figured out much. I haven't had custody very long. It's still a shock to all of us. I know the boys miss their mother and father, but they can't express it. I hate the loss for them. And I'm not sure I'm such a great choice as a parent. I've been totally dedicated to my career since I entered med school. Add to that how I've been filling in for Dr. Walters and it's tough. I don't want to let down my residents or the twins."

Bridget studied Ryder for a long moment. "Are you

sure you want to step in as their father? There are other options. There are people who would love to welcome the boys into their—"

"The boys are mine," he said, his jaw locking in resolution. "It may take me some time, but I'll figure it out. The boys are important to me. I held them minutes after they were born. I would do anything for them. We've just all been thrown a loop. We're all dealing with the loss of my brother and sister-in-law. I will be there for them. I will be."

She nodded slowly. "Okay. I'll try to help you with your nanny situation."

He paused and the electricity and emotion that flowed between them snapped and crackled. "Thank you."

She nodded. "It's late. I may need to borrow one of your shirts and I should talk to my security."

"No problem," he said, but the way he looked at her made her feel as if he'd much prefer she share his bed instead of taking the guest bed alone.

Bridget took a quick shower and brushed her teeth with the toothbrush Ryder supplied. Pushing her hands through the sleeves of the shirt he left in the guest bedroom for her, she drank in the fresh scent of the shirt. She climbed into bed, wondering what had possessed her to get involved in Ryder's situation and she remembered all the things she couldn't control or influence. Maybe, just maybe she could wave a magic wand in this one and help just a little.

It seemed only seconds after she fell asleep that she heard a knock at the door. She awakened, confused and disoriented. "Hello?"

"Bridget," a male voice said from the other side of the door. "It's me, Ryder."

The door opened a crack. "I just wanted you to know I'm leaving."

Her brain moved slowly. She was not at the hotel. She was at Ryder's townhome. "Um."

"The boys are still asleep."

She paused. "The boys?" She blinked. "Oh, the boys."

He came to the side of her bed. "Are you okay?"

"What time is it?"

"Five a.m."

"Is this when you usually leave for work?"

"Pretty much," he said.

"Okay," she said and tried to make her brain work. "What time do they usually get up?"

"Six or seven," he said. "I can try and call someone if—"

"No, I can do it," she said. "Just leave my door open so I can hear them."

"Are you sure?"

"Yes. Check in at lunchtime," she said.

"I can do that," he said and paused. "Did anyone ever tell you how beautiful you are when you're half-asleep?"

Unconsciously, her mouth lifted in a half smile. "I can't recall such a compliment."

"Nice to know I'm the first," he said, bending toward her and pressing his mouth against hers. Before she could say a word, he left.

Bridget wondered if she'd dreamed the kiss.

She fell back asleep for what must have been 30 seconds and she heard the sound of a baby's cry. It awakened her like cold water on her face. She sat upright, climbed out of bed and walked to the boys' room. She swung open the door to find Travis and Tyler sitting in their cribs and wailing.

"Hi, darlings," she said and went to Travis. "Good morning. It's a wonderful day to be a baby, isn't it?" She saw a twisty thing on the side of the crib and cranked it around. The mobile turned and music played. "Well, look at that," she said and touched the mobile.

Travis gave a few more sobs, but as soon as he looked upward, he quieted as the mobile turned.

Bridget felt a sliver of relief. "Good boy," she said and went to Tyler's bed and cranked up the mobile. Tyler looked upward and gave up his halfhearted cry, staring at the mobile.

Diaper change, she thought and took care of Travis. Then she took care of Tyler and hoisted both boys on her hips and went downstairs. She fed them, changed them again and propped them on a blanket in the den while she called her sister's friend for a reference for the best nanny agency in Dallas. Three hours later, she interviewed four nannies in between feeding the twins and changing more diapers and putting them down for a nap. When they fussed at nap time, she played a CD more repetitious than her brother's top-adviser's speech on a royal's duty. She'd heard that lecture too many times to count. The huge advantage to the babies' CD was that it included singing. Bridget wondered if she might have been more receptive to the lecture if the adviser had sung it.

The second prospective nanny was her favorite. She received letters of reference on her cell phone within an hour and sent a generous offer that was immediately accepted. After she checked on the boys, she ordered a nanny/babycam. Next in line, she would hire a relief nanny, but right now she needed a little relief of her own.

Bridget sank onto the couch and wondered when her day had felt so full. Even at this moment, she needed to use the bathroom, but she didn't have the energy to go. She glanced at herself, in her crumpled dress from yesterday with baby formula, baby food and liquid baby burp. That didn't include the drool.

Crazy, but the drool was sweet to her. How sick was that? But she knew the twins had drooled when they'd relaxed and trusted her.

She laughed quietly, a little hysterically. Anyone in their right mind would ask why she was working so hard to find a nanny for a doctor with two baby boys. Maybe a shrink could explain it, but these days, Bridget had a hard time turning down a cause of the heart. And Ryder and the boys had struck her straight in the heart with a deadly aim. She hoped, now, that she would feel some sort of relief.

Leaning back against the sofa with her bladder a little too full, she closed her eyes. Heaven help her, this baby stuff was exhausting.

Ryder left the office early, determined not to leave Bridget totally in the lurch with the boys. Stepping inside the front door, he found Bridget, mussed in the most alluring way, asleep on his couch.

She blinked, then her eyes widened. "Oh, excuse me. Just a second," she said, then raced down the hallway.

He listened carefully, automatically these days. A CD played over the baby monitor, but there were no other sounds. A double check never hurt, he thought, and strode upstairs to listen outside the nursery door.

Nothing. He opened the doorknob in slow motion and pushed the door open. Carefully stepping inside, he peeked into the cribs. Both boys were totally zoned out. He almost wondered if they were snoring but refused to check.

Backing out of the room, he returned downstairs to the den. Bridget was sipping from a glass of water.

"Are they still asleep?" she asked.

He nodded.

She grimaced. "I hate to say this. You have no idea how much I hate to say this, but we need to wake them or they'll be up all night. And I'm not staying tonight."

"Yeah," he said, but he was in no rush.

"I hired a nanny. She can start Monday. I've also ordered a baby/nannycam for your peace of mind. The next step is hiring a relief nanny because the twins are especially demanding at this age. Well, maybe they will be demanding at every age, but we have to deal with the present and the immediate future."

Ryder stared at her in disbelief. "How did you do that?"

She smiled. "I'm a fairy princess. I waved my magic wand," she said. "Actually I got into the best nanny agency in Dallas, used my title, interviewed four highly qualified women in between changing diapers, selected one applicant, received references, blah, blah, blah and it's done." She lifted her shoulders. "And now I'm done."

"I'm sure you are. In any other circumstance, I would invite you out to dinner for the evening."

"Lovely thought," she said. "But I feel extremely grungy. The opposite of glamorous. I'm going to my sister's ranch for the weekend. You can call me next week about all the doctors you want to send to Chantaine."

His lips twitched. "You don't really think I'm going to sell out one of my residents for this, do you?"

"Sell out is such a harsh term," she said with a scowl. "I believe it's more accurate that you're giving them an opportunity for hands-on experience in a beautiful environment with a compensation that allows them to concentrate on treatment rather than their debt."

He lifted an eyebrow. "Pretty good."

She shrugged. "It's the truth. My security is waiting to drive me to my sister's house. Can you take it from here?"

"Yes, I can. Do I have your number?" he asked. "For that dinner I promised."

She looked at him for a long, sexy moment that made him want to find a way to make her stay. "Some would say I'm more trouble than I'm worth," she said.

"They haven't seen you with twins," he said.

She smiled slightly and went to the kitchen. Out of curiosity, he followed and watched her scratch a number across the calendar tacked on the fridge. "Good enough?" she asked.

"Good enough," he said.

"Don't wait too long to call me, cowboy doctor," she said and walked toward the front door.

"I won't," he said, his gaze fixed on the sight of her amazing backside. "G'night, gorgeous."

She tossed a smile over her shoulder. "Same to you."

Bridget felt Valentina search her face. "Twin boys? Dr. Ryder? What does any of this have to do with you?"

It was Saturday morning. Noon, actually, as she sipped her tea and entered the world of the waking. "I didn't mean to get involved, but I didn't have a choice. I mean, the boys were orphaned. Ryder is grieving at the same time he's trying to take care of the babies. Trying to take on someone else's job because he's medically unable."

Tina stared at her in disbelief. "Are you sure you're okay? Maybe you need more rest."

Bridget laughed. "I'm sure I'll take another nap, but the story won't change tomorrow. It was something I had to do." She paused. "You understand that, don't you? When you have to fix it if you can?"

Tina's face softened and she covered Bridget's hand with hers. "Oh, sweetie, I'm so sorry," she said, shaking her head.

"For what?"

"The Devereaux fixing gene has kicked in," she said. "It's a gift and a plague."

"What do you mean?"

"I mean, you finally understand what it means to be a Devereaux Royal," she said, her expression solemn. "If you see a need, you try to fill it. If you see a pain, you try to heal it. It's your purpose. It's our purpose."

"So, I'm going to be doing stuff like this the rest of my life?" Bridget asked, appalled.

Tina nodded and Katiana banged on the tray of her high chair, clearly wanting more food.

"Oh, I hope not." Bridget didn't want to feel that much. She didn't want to get that emotionally involved. Surely, she could get this out of her system once and for all with Ryder and the babies and then get back to her true self in Italy.

Bridget sighed. "What I really want to do is wrap up

this doctor thing as soon as possible. I'm concerned it may not happen as quickly as I like."

"Why not?" Tina asked as she gave Katiana slices of peaches.

"I don't understand it all, but the way Ryder talks about it, going to Chantaine would be death for a physician's career. Sounds a bit overdramatic to me, but I need to get further information. In the meantime, Stefan has asked me to make some more official appearances, so I'll be traveling and spending more time in Dallas."

Tina frowned. "I don't like that," she said. "I thought you were going to spend most of your time here with me."

"I'll still be coming to the ranch as often as possible, but you know how Stefan is. He likes to maximize our efforts."

"How well I remember," Tina said with a groan. She dampened a clean cloth and wiped off Katiana's face and hands.

Katiana shook her adorable head and lifted her hands. "Up," she said.

"Of course, Your Highness," Tina said and gave her daughter a kiss as she lifted her from the chair.

Katiana immediately pointed at the floor. "Down."

"Please," Tina said.

Katiana paused.

"Please," Tina repeated. "Can you say that?"

"Psss," the toddler said.

"Close enough," Tina said with a laugh.

Bridget stared at her sister in jeans and a T-shirt and sometimes had to shake her head at the sight of her. "I'm just not used to seeing you quite so domesticated."

"I've been living here for more than two years now."

"Do you mind it? The work?" she asked. "At the palace, you could have had several nannies at your beck and call."

"I have Hildie the housekeeper, who may as well be Katiana's grandmother, and Zach. I like the simplicity of this life. Before I met Zach, I always felt like I was juggling a dozen priorities. Now between him and Katiana, the choice is easy."

"Must be nice," Bridget muttered as Hildie, Zach's longtime housekeeper, strode through the door carrying a bag of groceries.

"Well, hello, all Your Highlinesses. We've got a roomful of royalty today. Miss Tina, did you offer your sister some of that strawberry bread? Looks like you're having a late breakfast. Although that should come as no surprise considering when she got here last night," Hildie said, lifting her eyebrow.

Bridget wasn't quite certain how to take the stern-looking gray-haired woman. Tina insisted the woman had a heart of gold, but she seemed to rule the house with an iron hand. "Good morning, Miss—"

"Call me Hildie, and it's afternoon. Do you feel like some pancakes or a turkey sandwich? You looked pretty rough when you got in last night," Hildie said as she began to put away groceries.

"She was taking care of twin babies," Tina said, clearly still amazed.

Hildie's jaw dropped. "Twin babies," she said. "You?"

Bridget grimaced. "I know it's totally improbable. Hopefully I won't be put in that type of situation again."

"She was helping a doctor who had become a

guardian to his brother's two babies because the brother and sister-in-law were killed in an accident."

Hildie shook her head, her brow furrowing in deep sympathy. "That's terrible, just terrible. You did the right thing," she said to Bridget. "Let me fix you a pie. I'll fix you any kind you want."

Surprised, Bridget felt a rush of discomfort mixed with pleasure. "Oh, I don't need a pie. You're delightful to suggest it, but—"

"I insist," Hildie said.

Tina lifted her shoulders helplessly. "You're going to get a pie whether you like it or not. You may as well pick what you like, and I guarantee it will be the best pie you've eaten."

"Well, if you must, I would like the most decadent chocolate pie you can bake."

Hildie cackled with laughter. "Chocolate. You can tell the two of you are sisters. And you may try to hide it, but you have that fix-it compulsion just like your sister."

"I don't have that compulsion," Bridget insisted. "It's temporary. Like a virus. As soon as I take my long break in Italy, I'll be cured."

Hildie laughed again and shot her a look of sympathy. "Don't worry, Your Highliness. It may take a while, but you'll figure it out."

Bridget frowned because it seemed that Hildie knew something she didn't. Hmm. The prospect didn't please her, but the chocolate would help.

Chapter Three

Three nights later, Ryder met Bridget at an exclusive Mediterranean restaurant in Dallas. He remembered she'd said she preferred Mediterranean and Italian food. With the Dallas skyline outside the window beside them, he couldn't look anywhere but at her. Her blue eyes sparkled with a combination of sensuality and warmth. Her black dress—yet another one—dipped into a V that cupped her beautiful breasts and her lips were, again, red.

"Thank you for joining me," he said after they'd placed their order.

"Thank you for inviting me. Who's watching the twins?" she asked.

"A neighbor and her daughter. I'm paying double. Amazing how easy it was for them to commit when I said that," he said.

She laughed. "They're adorable but exhausting. How was the new nanny?"

"Scary efficient. This was her first day and she's already whipping all of us into shape," he said, amazed at how good he felt just to be with Bridget.

"Good. Next step is to get a backup," she said and took a sip of wine. "In the meantime, about Chantaine's medical program…"

He stifled a groan. "Do we have to discuss business?"

"Briefly," she said and lifted an eyebrow. "Remember that we held our discussion while the twins were screaming *after* I had cared for them during your meeting and—"

"Okay, okay," he said. "Do you want me to be blunt?"

"I would love it," she said, leaning forward and propping her chin on her hands.

"The truth is, there's no true professional advantage for the residents to go to Chantaine after they graduate. There's no extra education, association with an expert, or certification."

"So money is not enough," she said.

"No," he said.

"Hmm." She tilted her head. "So the whole game would change if Chantaine could offer exposure to a noted expert in a particular field?"

He nodded.

She took another sip of her wine. "Thank you."

He could tell her brain was already racing. "You're plotting and planning," he said.

She smiled, her sexy red lips lifting upward, sending a sensual heat through his veins. "Yes, I am. I'll figure something out. It's the Devereaux way."

"I did an internet search on you," he admitted. "You've *mostly* stayed out of trouble. How did you manage that?"

"I'm flattered. Of course, I did research on you right after the cocktail party. How did I stay out of trouble?" she asked. "It's all relative. My sisters did me a huge favor. I wouldn't wish it on her, but Ericka went to rehab, and then after that, Tina got pregnant. What a scandal. So my little tumbles—"

"Like the time you got smashed at the nightclub in Chantaine and made a scene—"

"That was Stefan's fault. Eve was with me and he couldn't stand the fact that she wasn't with him." She waved her hand. "But I won't fault him too much. He'd just discovered he had a baby from an earlier affair and was trying to work out his relationship with Eve."

"I remember reading an article about some sort of incident. A gang. She was hurt."

He stopped when he saw her gaze darken with emotion.

"She saved my life and nearly lost her own," Bridget said quietly as she ran her finger around the top of her glass. "It all happened so fast. I wish I had responded differently. She was hurt. She almost died." She lifted her glass and took a quick sip. "It was wrong. Her life shouldn't have been put in jeopardy for my sake."

He was shocked at the stark guilt he saw on her face. "These things happen. Decisions are made in microseconds. She's a Texas girl. She acted on instinct."

She bit her lip. "Maybe I need to learn some of those Texas-girl instincts," she muttered.

"Your instincts are pretty damn good. You took care of the twins when we were in a jam," he said.

"That's different," she said.

"Not as far as I can see. I won't lie to you. I can't make any promises about sending doctors to Chantaine. On the other hand, I've thought about having you in my bed way too much. I wish I could say it's just because you've got a killer body and I've done without, but the truth is, there's something else about you that gets me going."

Her lips parted in startled disbelief. "I—" She broke off and shook her head. "I don't know what to say."

"You don't have to say anything. I just wanted you to know," he said.

She met his gaze and he could tell she was undecided. He saw want and hesitation, and he understood it, but he was driven to find a way to get her to meet him halfway.

After a delicious dinner, Ryder drove Bridget to her hotel and insisted on walking her to her room. "You know security is watching me," she said as they stood outside her door.

"Do you want to step inside your room?"

An illicit thrill raced through her. Her guard would report to Stefan and he would fuss. She would dodge his calls the same way she had after spending the night at Ryder's house. What a hassle. "For just a moment," she said and slid her key card into the lock.

Ryder pushed open the door. Seconds later, she felt her back against the door and his mouth on hers.

"Do you know what your red mouth does to me?"

he muttered and plundered her lips. He slid his tongue into her mouth, tasting her, taking her.

Her heart slammed against her ribs. She couldn't resist the urge to lift her fingers to his hair and scalp.

He groaned in approval and rocked his hips against hers.

Bridget gasped, her breath locking somewhere between her lungs and throat. Somehow, someway, she craved his warmth and strength. His passion and need struck her at her core.

"I want you," he said. "You want me. Let me stay for a while."

A terrible wicked temptation rolled through her. If he stayed, he would fill her and take her away from her uncertainty and emptiness. She knew he could take care of her, if only for a little while.

He French-kissed her, sending her around the world at least a couple of times.

"You want me to stay?" he asked, sliding his mouth down over her ear.

She inhaled, grasping for sanity. Closing her eyes, she tried to concentrate. "Yesandno," she said, running the words together. She dipped her head so that her forehead rested against his chin. "This is a little fast."

He gave a heavy, unsatisfied sigh. "Yeah, it is. But it's strong."

She nodded. "Sorry," she whispered.

"It's okay," he said cradling the back of her head. "It wouldn't work out anyway."

"Why is that?" she asked, leaning back to look at him.

"I'm a doctor. You're a princess," he said.

"So?" she asked.

"The two don't mix," he said. "And never will. Sweet dreams, Your Highness."

He left and Bridget stared at the door, frowning. *Why couldn't they mix?* Not that she *wanted* them to mix. And the *sweet dreams* thing really grated on her. That was what Eve had often said. It had seemed so sweet when she'd said it. Not so with Ryder. Bridget snarled. He was gone. Good riddance.

Ryder heard a knocking sound and shook his head as he glanced up during the meeting he was in to discuss the performance of the residents.

Dr. Wayne Hutt, Ryder's nemesis, knocked on the table again. "Dr. McCall?" he said. "Anyone home?"

"Pardon me," Ryder said in a crisp voice. "I was studying my notes."

"Apology accepted," Hutt said. "Drs. Robinson and Graham are having attendance issues."

"Dr. Robinson is concerned about the welfare of his family in rural Virginia and Dr. Graham's wife has just gotten pregnant," Ryder said. "They just need a little time to refocus. It won't be a problem."

"How can you be sure?" Hutt challenged.

Ryder fought his antipathy for his associate. "I'm sure," he said. "Just as Dr. Gordon Walters would be sure," he said, pulling rank because everyone knew Dr. Walters trusted Ryder over anyone else.

Hutt gave an odd combination of a frown and grimace.

Dr. James Williams, chief of everything, nodded.

"We'll give these two interns two weeks to make adjustments. Dr. McCall, you'll speak to them?"

"Yes, sir."

Seven minutes later, the meeting ended, thank God. He returned to his office and sent emails to Drs. Robinson and Graham to set up appointments. He answered another fifty emails and stood to make late rounds with his patients.

A knock sounded outside his door and Dr. Hutt walked inside. "Hey, Ryder. Late night. I'm surprised you can do this with the twins."

Ryder resisted the urge to grind his teeth. "I've hired a new nanny and am getting new backup. Thanks for your concern. I need to do late rounds."

"Just a minute," Hutt said. "How's Dr. Walters doing? No one's talking."

"He's working through his recovery. These things take time," Ryder hedged.

"That's pretty vague," Hutt said.

"You know I can't discuss the confidential status of patients," he said.

"But Walters isn't really your patient," Hutt continued.

"He's my mentor and friend, the closest thing I've had to a father since my own father died when I was a kid. I'm not discussing his condition," Ryder said.

"It must not be good," Hutt said. "You know if the twins are too much for you, I'll be glad to step in and help."

Ryder just bet Hutt would like to step in and *help*. What Hutt really wanted was a promotion. What Hutt really wanted was to snatch Walters's position away from Ryder. Although Ryder hated that Walters couldn't fulfill his duties any longer.

"Thanks for the offer," he said.

"Seriously, Ryder. I have a wife and a child. The wife is the critical element. She makes it easy for me to do my job. When you don't have a wife…"

"I have a good new nanny," he said.

"It's not the same as a wife," Hutt counseled.

"Hmm. See you. Good night," he said and headed out the door. What Hutt didn't understand was that Ryder had never had any intention of getting married and having children. He'd observed his parents' disastrous marriage, his father's death and his mother's subsequent descent into alcoholism and death.

After that, Ryder had resolved that he wanted to heal people. Bag the personal relationships, with the exception of his brother and his family. His family became his patients, and after he completed his residency, his family included the new residents. And always Dr. Walters. He would never take a wife. His mind wandered to a visual of Bridget the last time he'd seen her, her eyes catlike with sensuality, her mouth soft and sensual, taking him into her. His mouth into her. When he really wanted to give her a lot more.

Ryder swore under his breath. This was all libido. He'd taken care of this issue before with other women doctors as career-driven as he was. No-ties sex provided a release that allowed him to do his job. Maintaining his focus on his profession and the twins was the most important thing. Bridget was just a distraction.

Bridget wandered around the medical association meeting and was bummed that Ryder wasn't there. He was probably taking care of the twins. She felt a deep tug of sympathy and quickly tried to brush it aside. Ryder didn't want her sympathy. They would never work. Remember? She covered her irritation with a smile as she nodded at someone else she didn't know.

Halfway through the evening, the shrimp bowl was refilled and Bridget put a few on her plate.

"I always wait for the refill at these things," a distinguished older man said to her.

She nodded in agreement. "I agree. Fresh is better. Bridget Devereaux," she said, extending her free hand.

"Dr. James Williams, University Hospital," he said shaking her hand. "Are you a pharmaceutical sales rep?"

She opened her mouth and it took a moment to speak. She smiled. "Not exactly. I'm representing the country of Chantaine. Very small country in the Mediterranean. We're trying to recruit more doctors. We're offering complimentary living expenses and paying special scholarships in addition to salary for a two-year stay."

Dr. Williams lifted his white eyebrows. "Really? I'll have to speak to my physician in charge of residents about that. Perhaps a couple of them could benefit from that."

"I would appreciate that very much. I'm sure you're a very busy man. Would you mind if I touch base with you in a week or so?"

"Not at all," he said. "Some of our residents have money challenges. Don't we all in this economy?"

"So true," she said. "Are you the speaker tonight?"

He shook his head. "No, I'm lucky. Eat and leave."

She laughed. "Don't rub it in," she said.

He laughed in return. "Tell me your name again. I don't want to forget."

"Bridget Devereaux," she said, deliberately leaving out her title. "I represent Chantaine. I'm honored to meet you."

"My pleasure to meet you, Miss Devereaux," he said, and ate his shrimp cocktail.

Bridget worked the room the rest of the night and arranged a visit to the pediatric wing at Texas Medical Center to make a public service announcement for public health. She also met several doctors who wanted to pursue a more personal relationship, but she demurred at the same time that she gave them her card which contained a number for her assistant.

By the time the evening was done, her feet were also done. Her mind wandered to Ryder and the babies, but she tried to push her thoughts aside. With a glass of white wine in her hand, she kicked off her high heels and watched television in her suite at the hotel.

She closed her eyes. Soon enough she would be in Italy with a gorgeous Italian man keeping her company. She smiled at the image, but soon another image flashed in its place. Ryder, sans shirt, stood before her and dragged her into his arms and began to make love to her. He was so hot that smoke rose between them, but the sensation of his skin against hers made her dizzy. His kiss made her knees weak. He made her want in a way she never had….

She felt herself sinking into the couch, her body warm and pliable. And alone.

Bridget blinked and sat up against the couch. This was just wrong. He'd already said they wouldn't work because of who he was, because of who she was. A part of her rebelled against the notion one moment. The next, she didn't. She didn't have room for this drama in her life. She had goals. She had Italy in her future.

Bridget washed her face and brushed her teeth, determined to put Ryder from her mind. As she fell asleep, though, she dreamed of Ryder and the boys.

A few days later, Ryder followed up on a surgery patient midday. The young man had been admitted to the E.R. with appendicitis. Ryder had operated and needed to give his stamp of approval for the teen to be discharged. He was stopped because there was filming in the pediatric unit.

Slightly irritated, he checked his text messages on his cell and answered a few.

"She's a princess making a video," one nurse said to another.

He snapped his head up at the comment. "Princess?" he repeated.

"Yes," the nurse said. "But she's very nice. Not at all snooty. I got her coffee and she was very grateful. More than a lot of doctors."

"She wasn't trying to save lives," Ryder said.

The nurse shrugged. "Anyone can say please and thank you, and she did."

Minutes later, Bridget appeared, lighting up the room with her smile. The chief of Pediatrics accompanied her, clearly dazzled.

"Thank you," she said. "Thank you so much from Chantaine and me. You have been wonderful."

"Isn't she wonderful? Now *that* is a princess," the nurse said.

Ryder wanted to make a wry, cynical response, but he was too busy staring at Bridget. And the damned pediatric chief. She seemed to glow. He remembered how she'd felt in his arms, how that wicked red mouth had felt against his. He remembered how she'd made him smile. Not many people had managed to do that during the last few months.

She squeezed the pediatrics chief's arm, then glanced around the room and waved. Her gaze locked with his and he felt a surge of need all the way down to his feet. It was sexual, but more, and confused the hell out of him. She gave a quick little wave and returned her attention to the pediatric chief.

Ryder felt an inexplicable surge of jealousy. *Where the hell had that come from?* Pushing it aside, he continued to his patient's room for the final exam. Less than five minutes later, he headed down the hallway toward his office. Rounding a corner, he nearly plowed into Bridget and Dr. Ware, the pediatrics chief, who was chatting her up. His body language said he wanted to eat her with a spoon. His hand placed on the wall above her head, he leaned toward her. Ryder fought the crazy urge to push him away, but turned his head instead.

"Ryder. Dr. McCall," Bridget said.

He slowed his steps and turned around and nodded in her direction.

"How are you? The twins? The new nanny?" she asked, her gaze searching his.

Ware stepped beside her. "Whoa, she knows a lot about you, McCall. How did that happen?"

Ryder shrugged. "Just lucky, I guess. I'm good. The twins are good and the new nanny is fantastic. I could say I owe you my life, but I'd be afraid you'd take it."

She shot him a look of mock offense. "You know better than that. Besides, it's not your life that I want," she said with a laugh.

Ware looked from one of them to the other, clearly curious. "What *does* she want? And why in the world wouldn't you give it to her?"

"She wants my residents," he said, meeting her gaze.

"After they've completed your program," she insisted. "Plus, I only want to *borrow* them for a couple of years, and they'll be well compensated."

"You could throw her one or—" Dr. Ware's pager sounded. "Please excuse me. I need to go. You have my card, Your Highness. Give me a call. Anytime," he said with a hopeful smile and rushed away.

Bridget sighed and turned to Ryder. "Are you going to do the civilized thing and ask me to join you for lunch?"

"If I haven't been civilized before, why should I start now?" Ryder retorted because Bridget made him feel anything but civilized.

"I suppose because you owe me your life," she said with a glint in her eyes.

He gave a muffled chuckle. "Okay, come along. I better warn you that lunch won't last longer than fifteen minutes."

"Ah, so you're into quickies. What a shame," she said and began to walk.

"I didn't say that," he said, but resisted the urge to pull at his collar which suddenly felt too tight.

"I can't say I'm surprised. All evidence points in that direction."

"How did we get on this subject?" he asked.

"You said you wouldn't last more than fifteen minutes," she said, meeting his gaze with eyes so wide and guileless that he wondered how she did it.

"I said *lunch* won't last—" He broke when he saw her smile. "Okay, you got me on that one. I hope you don't mind cafeteria food."

"Not at all," she said as they walked into the cafeteria.

He noticed several people stared in their direction, but she seemed to ignore it. They each chose a couple dishes and he paid for both, then guided her to a less-occupied table at the back of the room. "How did your video go today?"

"Hopefully, well. I interviewed Dr. Ware about preventative health for children. I also need to do one for adults. But enough about that. How are the twins?" she asked, clearly eager for information.

"I think the new nanny is making a big difference for them. This is the most calm I've seen them since I took custody of them," he said. "The nanny also suggested that I do some extra activities with them, but I haven't worked that into the schedule yet."

"What kind of activities?" she asked, and took a bite of her chicken.

"Swimming," he said then lowered his voice. *"Baby yoga."*

"Oh. Do you take yoga?" she asked and sipped her hot tea.

"Never in my life," he said. "The nanny seems to

think this would increase bonding between the three of us."

"That makes you uncomfortable," she said.

He shrugged. "I hadn't planned on having kids. I guess I'm still adjusting, too."

"You've been through a lot. Perhaps you should see a therapist," she said.

"We're doing okay now," he said defensively.

"I don't suggest it as an insult. The palace is always giving us head checks especially since my sister Ericka had her substance-abuse problem. I'm surprised it's not required in this situation."

"A social worker has visited a few times to check on things. She actually suggested the same thing," he said reluctantly. "She said I need to make sure I'm having fun with the boys instead of it being all work."

"There you go," she said. "I think it's a splendid idea. You just seem incredibly overburdened and miserable."

"Thank you for that diagnosis, Your Highness," he said drily and dug into his dry salmon filet. "Funny, a friend of mine said something similar recently."

"We all have to protect against burnout. I would say you're more in danger of it than most."

"Is there such a thing as princess burnout?" he asked.

"Definitely. That's what happened to my sister Valentina. She carried the load too long."

"And what are you doing to prevent burnout?"

"I have an extended break planned in my future. In the meantime, I try to make sure I get enough rest and solitude whenever possible. As soon as I wrap up the doctor assignment, I'll get a break. I'm hoping you'll toss me one or two of your residents as Dr. Ware suggested to get the ball rolling."

"It's going to be more difficult than that," he said.

"I don't see why it needs to be. It's not as if I'm seriously asking for your top neurosurgeons. We would love a general practitioner or family doctor. In fact, we would prefer it."

"You and the rest of the world. We actually have a shortage of family physicians, too."

"Again, I'm only asking to *borrow* them."

"What do you think of Dr. Ware?" he asked, changing the subject again.

"He's lovely. Unlike you, he's totally enchanted with my position and title."

"Part of my charm. Part of the reason you find me irresistible."

"You flatter yourself," she said.

"Do I?" he challenged. "You've missed me."

"Of course I haven't. You already said nothing would work between us. Of course, that was after you tried to shag me against the hotel door. I mean, you obviously have the attention span of a fruit fly when it comes to women and—"

He closed his hand over hers. "Will you shut up for a minute?"

Surprisingly, she did.

"I dream about you whenever I get the rare opportunity to sleep. I've dialed your number and hung up too many times to count. You can't want to get involved with me right now."

"It's not for you to tell me what I can and can't want. Lord knows, everyone else does that. Don't you start."

"Okay," he said wearily.

"So what are you going to do about it?" she challenged.

If he said what he *wanted* to do, he could be arrested. "I think I'll show instead of tell," he said and watched with satisfaction as her throat and face bloomed with color. He wondered if her blush extended to the rest of her body. It would be fun to find out.

Chapter Four

Two days later, Bridget's cell phone rang and her heart went pitter-patter at the number on the caller ID. "Hello," she said in a cool voice.

"Hello to you, Your Highness. How are you?" Ryder asked.

"I'm actually getting ready to make an appearance for a children's art program in Dallas," she said, smiling at the people who were waiting for her.

"Okay, I'll make this quick. Are you free tonight?"

She rolled her eyes. The man clearly had no idea how many demands were placed on her once people got word she was in the area. "I'm not often free but can sometimes make adjustments. What did you have in mind?"

"Swimming," he said.

"Excuse me?" she said.

"Swimming with the twins and pizza," he said.

"The pizza had better be fabulous. Ciao," she said and disconnected the call, but she felt a crazy surge of happiness zing through her as she followed the museum representatives inside the room where the children and press awaited.

Bridget gave a brief speech about the importance of art at all levels of society and dipped her hands and feet in purple paint. She stepped on a white sheet of paper, then pressed her handprints above and finished with her autograph.

The crowd applauded and she was technically done, but she stayed longer to talk to the children as they painted and worked on various projects. Their warmth and responsiveness made her feel less jaded, somehow less weary. Who would have thought it possible?

After extensive rearrangements of her schedule, Bridget put on her swimsuit and had second thoughts. What had possessed her to agree to join Ryder for a swim class when she was in a nearly naked state? She didn't have a perfectly slim body. In fact, if honest, she was curvy with pouches. Her bum was definitely larger than her top.

Her stomach clenched. Oh, bloody hell, she might as well be thirteen years old again. Forget it, she told herself. It wasn't as if anything could happen. She and Ryder would have two six-month-old chaperones.

Within forty-five minutes, she and Ryder stood in a pool with Tyler and Travis. Tyler stuck to her like glue, his eyes wide and fearful. "It's okay," she coaxed, bobbing gently in the water.

Ryder held Travis, who was screaming bloody murder.

"Are we having fun yet?" he asked, holding his god-son securely.

"Should we sing?" she asked, trying not to be distracted by Ryder's broad shoulders and well-muscled arms and chest. For bloody's sake, when did the man have time to work out?

"They would throw us out," he said. "You look good in water."

She felt a rush of pleasure. "Thank you. Is Travis turning purple?"

"I think it's called rage," he said.

"Would you like to switch off for a moment?"

"Are you sure?" he asked doubtfully.

She nodded. "Let me give him a go," she said.

Tyler protested briefly at the exchange, then attached himself to Ryder. Travis continued to scream, so she lowered her mouth to his ear and began to quietly sing a lullaby from her childhood. Travis cried, but the sound grew less intense. She kept singing and he made sad little yelps, then finally quieted.

"Aren't you the magic one?" Ryder said.

"Luck," she said and cooed at the baby, swirling him around in the water. "Doesn't this feel good?" she murmured.

By the end of class, they'd switched off again and Travis was cackling and shrieking with joy as he splashed and kicked and Ryder whirled him around in the water.

As soon as they stepped from the pool, they wrapped the boys in snuggly towels. Ryder rubbed Travis's arms. She did the same with Tyler and he smiled at her. Her heart swelled at his sweetness. "You are such a good boy. Isn't he?" she said to Ryder.

"You bet," Ryder said and pressed his mouth against Tyler's chubby cheek, making a buzzing sound. Tyler chortled with joy.

"That sound is magic," she said.

Ryder nodded as he continued to rub Travis. "Yeah, it is." His glance raked her from head to toe and he shook his head. "You look pretty damn good."

Bridget felt a warmth spread from her belly to her chest and face, down her legs, all the way to her toes. "It's just been a long time for you," she said and turned away to put some clothes on Tyler.

A second later, she felt Ryder's bare chest against her back. An immediate visceral response rocked through her and she was torn between jumping out of her skin and melting. "Yeah, it has," he said. "But that shouldn't make you so damn different from every other woman I've met."

Her stomach dipped. "Stop flattering me," she said. "Get your baby dressed. You don't want him chilled."

After pizza and a raucous bath time, Ryder and Bridget rocked the babies and put them to bed. Ryder would have preferred to usher Bridget into his bed and reacquaint himself with the curves he'd glimpsed in the pool, but he would have to bide his time. Hopefully not too long, he told himself as his gaze strayed to the way her hips moved in her cotton skirt. He'd thought he was so smart getting her out of most of her clothes by inviting her to the baby swimming class. Now he would live with those images all night long.

"Wine?" he asked, lifting a bottle from the kitchen before he joined her in the den.

She had sunk onto the sofa and leaned her head back against it, unintentionally giving him yet another seductive photo for his mental collection. One silky leg crossed over the other while the skirt hugged her hips. The V-neck of her black shirt gave him just a glimpse of creamy cleavage. For once, her lips were bare, but that didn't stop him from wanting to kiss her.

Her eyes opened to slight slits shrouded with the dark fan of her eyelashes. "One glass," she said. "I think everyone will sleep well tonight."

Speak for yourself, he thought wryly and poured her wine. He allowed himself one glass because he wasn't on call.

"It's amazing how much they can scream, isn't it?" she said as he sat beside her.

"They save up energy lying around all the time. It's not like they can play football or baseball yet."

"Have you thought about which sport you'll want them to pursue?" she asked.

"Whatever keeps them busy and tired. If they're busy and tired, they won't be as likely to get into trouble," he said.

"So that's the secret," she said with a slow smile. "Did that work for you?"

"Most of the time. I learned at a young age that I wanted a different life than the life my parents had."

"Hmm, at least you knew your parents," she said.

"Can't say knowing my father was one of my strong points."

"Well, you know what they say, if you can't be a good example, be a terrible warning."

He chuckled slightly and relaxed next to her. "I don't want to be the same kind of father he was. Drunk. Neglectful. Bordering on abusive."

"You couldn't be those things," she said.

"Why not? You've heard the saying, an apple doesn't fall too far from the tree."

"You've already fallen a long way from that so-called tree," she said. "Plus, you may be fighting some of your feelings, but you love those boys." She lifted her hand to his jaw. "You have a good heart. I liked that about you from the first time I met you."

"And I thought it was my singing voice," he said and lowered his mouth to hers, reveling in the anticipation he felt inside and saw in her eyes.

She tasted like a delicious combination of red wine, tiramisu and something forbidden that he wasn't going to resist. Ryder was certain he could resist her if he wanted. If there was one thing Ryder possessed, it was self-discipline. The quality had been necessary to get him through med school, residency and even more so now in his position at the hospital and with the twins.

For now, though, Ryder had decided he didn't want to resist Bridget. With her lush breasts pressing against his chest, discipline was the last thing on his mind. She was so voluptuously female from her deceptively airy attitude to her curvy body. He slid one of his hands through her hair as she wiggled against him.

A groan of pleasure and want rose from his throat as she deepened the kiss, drawing his tongue into her mouth. The move echoed what he wanted to be doing with the rest of his body and hers. He wrapped his hands around her waist. He slid one down to her hips and the other upward to just under her breast.

He was so hard that he almost couldn't breathe. She was so soft, so feminine, so hot. With every beat of his heart, he craved her. He wanted to consume her, to slide inside her....

Ryder slid his hand to her breast, cupping its fullness. Her nipple peaked against his palm. The fire inside him rising, he tugged a few buttons of her blouse loose and slipped his hand under her bra, touching her bare skin, which made him want to touch every inch of her. He couldn't remember wanting to inhale a woman before.

The next natural step would be to remove her clothes and his and after that, caress her with his hands and mouth. After that, he wanted to slide inside her.... She would be so hot, so wet....

All he wanted was to be as close to her as humanly possible.

From some peripheral area of his brain, he heard a knock and then another. Her body and soul called to him. He took her mouth in another deep kiss.

Another knock sounded, this time louder, but Ryder was determined to ignore it.

Suddenly his front door opened and Marshall burst into the room.

"Whoa," Marshall said. "Sorry to interrupt."

Ryder felt Bridget pull back and hastily arrange her shirt. "Who—" she said in a breathless voice.

"My best friend from high school, Marshall," Ryder said. "He has a key," he continued in a dark voice.

Marshall lifted his hands. "Hey, I called and you

didn't answer. I started getting worried. You almost always answer at night. We've had a beer three times during the last week." His friend stared at Bridget and gave a low whistle. "And who do we have here?"

Irritated, Ryder scowled. "Show a little respect. Prin—" He stopped when Bridget pinched his arm. Staring at her in disbelief, he could see that she didn't want him to reveal her title. "Bridget Devereaux, this is Marshall Bailey."

His friend moved forward and extended his hand. Bridget stood and accepted the courtesy.

"Nice to meet you, Bridget," Marshall said. "It's a relief to see Ryder with a woman."

Embarrassment slammed through Ryder and he also stood. "Marshall," he said in a warning tone.

"I didn't mean that the way it sounded. The poor guy hasn't had much company except me and the twins." Marshall cleared his throat. "How did you two meet anyway?"

"Okay, enough, Mr. Busybody. As you can see, I'm fine, so you can leave."

"Oh no, that's not necessary," Bridget said and glanced at her watch. "I really should be leaving. I have an early flight tomorrow."

"Where?" Ryder asked.

"Chicago. They have a teaching hospital. I'll be meeting with the hospital chief to present the proposal for Chantaine's medical exchange."

"Oh," he said, surprised at the gut punch of disappointment he felt when he should feel relieved. "I guess this means you've given up on our residents."

"No, but you haven't been at all receptive. My brother

Stefan has instructed me to explore other possibilities. Your program was our first choice due to the quality of your residents and also the fact that you have so many family doctors and prevention specialists. But because you're unwilling to help…"

"For Pete's sake, Ryder, help the woman out," Marshall said and moved forward. "Is there anything I can do?"

Marshall was really getting on Ryder's nerves. "Not unless you have a medical degree and are licensed to practice," Ryder said.

"I believe my driver is here. Thank you for an action-packed evening," she said with a smile full of sexy amusement.

Ryder would have preferred a different kind of action. "I'll walk you to the car," he said, then shot a quick glance at Marshall. "I'll be back in a minute."

Ryder escorted Bridget to the limo waiting at the curb. A man stood ready to open the door for her. Ryder was disappointed as hell that she was headed out of town. Stupid. "So how long will you be gone?" he asked.

She lifted a dark eyebrow and her lips tilted in a teasing grin. "Are you going to miss me, Dr. McCall?"

His gut twisted. "That would be crazy. The only thing I've been missing for the last month is sleep," he lied.

"Oh, well, maybe you'll get lucky and get some extra sleep while I'm gone. Ta-ta," she said and turned toward the limo.

He caught her wrist and drew her back against him. The man at the car door took a step toward them, but she waved her hand. "Not necessary, Raoul."

"You must enjoy tormenting me," he said.

"Me?" she said, her blue eyes wide with innocence. "How could I possibly have the ability to torment you?"

"I don't know, but you sure as hell do," he muttered and kissed her, which only served to make him hotter. He turned her own words on her. "So, Your Highness, what are you going to do about it?"

She gave a sharp intake of breath and her eyes darkened as if her mind were working the same way as his. She bit her lip. "I can call you when I return from Chicago."

"Do that," he said.

Ryder returned to his house to find Marshall lounging on the sofa and drinking a glass of red wine. "This isn't bad," he said.

"Glad you like it. In the future, give me a call before you drop in. Okay?"

Marshall looked injured. "I did call you. You just didn't answer." He shook his head and gave a low whistle. "And now I understand why. That's one hot babe, and she reeks money. A limo came to pick her up? You sure know how to pick 'em. How did you meet her?"

"In an elevator," Ryder said, not wanting to give away too many details. As much as he liked his old friend, Ryder knew Marshall could gossip worse than an old lady.

"Really?" Marshall said, dumbfounded. "An elevator. Was it just you and her? Did you do anything— adventurous?"

"Not the way you're thinking," Ryder said in a dry tone, although if it had been just him and Bridget in that elevator without the twins, his mind would have gone in the same direction.

"Well, I'm glad you're finally getting some action," Marshall said.

Ryder swore. "I'd say you pretty much nixed that tonight. Between you and the twins, who needs birth control?"

Marshall chuckled. "Sorry, bud, better luck next time. I thought I'd see if Suzanne was hanging around tonight. She stays late for you sometimes."

Realization struck Ryder. "You didn't come by to see me. You came to see my nanny. I'm telling you now. Keep your hands off my nanny. She's not your type."

"Who says?"

"I say."

"Why isn't she my type? She's pretty. She's nice," he said.

"She's six years older than you are," Ryder said.

"So? She doesn't look it. She's got a fresh look about her and she's sweet. Got a real nice laugh," Marshall said.

"I'm not liking what I'm hearing," Ryder said, stepping between Marshall and the television. "So far, Suzanne is the perfect nanny. I don't want you messing with her. The boys and I need her."

"She's an adult. She can decide if she wants me to mess with her," he said with a shrug.

"Marshall," he said in a dead-serious voice. "She's not like your dime-a-dozen girls running fast and loose. She's not used to a guy like you who'll get her in the sack and leave her like yesterday's garbage."

Marshall winced. "No need to insult me. I've had a few long-term relationships."

"Name them," Ryder challenged.

"Well, there was that redhead, Wendy. She and I saw each other for at least a couple of years."

"She lived out of town, didn't she?" Ryder asked. "How many other women were you seeing at the same time?"

Marshall scowled. "Okay, what about Sharona? We lived together."

"For how long?"

"Seven weeks, but—"

"Enough said. Keep your paws off Suzanne."

Marshall slugged down the rest of the wine and stood. "You know, I'm not a rotten guy."

"Never said you were."

"I just haven't ever found the right girl," Marshall said.

"As long as you and I understand that Suzanne is not the right girl for you, everything will be fine."

Three days later, Bridget returned from her trip to Chicago. She hadn't snagged any doctors, but she'd persuaded one of the specialists she'd met to visit Chantaine and offer lectures and demonstrations. She was getting closer to her goal. She could feel it. Even though what she really wanted to do tonight was soak in a tub and watch television, she was committed to attend a charity event for Alzheimer's with the governor's son, who was actually quite a bit older than she was. Part of the job, she told herself as she got ready. She thought about calling Ryder, but every time she thought about him, she felt a jumpiness in her stomach. Bridget wasn't sure how far she wanted to go with him because she knew she would be leaving Dallas as soon as she accomplished her mission.

There was something about the combination of his strength and passion that did things to her. It was exciting. And perplexing.

Preferring to have her own chauffeur, Bridget met Robert Goodwin, the governor's son, in the lobby of her hotel. He was a distinguished-looking man in his mid-forties who reminded her of one of her uncles. She decided that was how she would treat him.

Her bodyguard Raoul, who occasionally played double duty in making introductions, stepped forward. "Your Highness, Robert Goodwin."

She nodded and extended her hand. "Lovely to meet you, Mr. Goodwin. Thank you for escorting me to an event that will raise awareness for such an important cause."

"My pleasure, Your Highness," he said, surprising her when he brought her hand to his mouth. "Please call me Robert. May I say that you look breathtaking?"

"Thank you very much, Robert. Shall we go?"

By the time they arrived at the historical hall, Bridget concluded that Mr. Goodwin's intentions were not at all uncle-like and she prepared herself for a sticky evening. Cameras flashed as they exited the limo and Mr. Goodwin appeared to want to linger for every possible photo as he bragged about her title to the reporters.

"Everyone is excited to have a real princess at the event tonight. People paid big bucks to sit at our table."

"I'm delighted I could help the cause." Sometimes it amazed her that a single spermatozoa had determined her status. And that spermatozoa had originated from a cheating jerk of a man who had never gotten her first name right. Her father.

"Would you join me in a dance?" Robert said, his gaze dipping to her cleavage.

"Thank you, but I need to powder my nose," she said. "Can you tell me where the ladies' room is?"

Robert blinked. "I believe it's down the hall to the left."

"Excuse me," she said and headed for the restroom, fully aware that Raoul was watching. She wondered if she could plead illness. After stalling for several moments, she left and slowly walked toward her table. Halfway there, Ryder stepped in front of her.

"Busy as ever," he said.

Her heart raced at the sight of him. "So true. I arrived back in town this afternoon and had to turn right around to get ready for this event."

"With the governor's son," Ryder said, clearly displeased.

"He could be my uncle," she said.

"Bet that's not what he's thinking," Ryder countered.

She grimaced and shrugged. "It's not the first time I've had to manage unwelcome interest, and if my appearance generates additional income for this good cause..."

"True," he said, his eyes holding a misery that grabbed at her.

"What brings you here?"

"Dr. Walters. He has had an impact on hundreds of doctors, but now he can't recognize himself in the mirror."

"I'm so sorry," she said, her heart hurting at the

expression on his face. "Seeing you, hearing you, makes me glad I came. I'm ashamed to confess that I was tempted to cancel because I was so tired after returning from Chicago."

His gaze held hers for a long emotional moment. "I'm glad you didn't give in to your weariness this time."

"Even though I have to face Mr. Anything-but-Good Robert Goodwin," she said.

"Give me a sign and I'll have your back," he said.

She took a deep breath. "That's good to know. I can usually handle things. This isn't the first time."

His gaze swept over her from head to toe and back again. "That's no surprise."

Her stomach dipped and she cleared her throat. "I should get back to my table. I'm told people paid to sit with me. I'm sure it has nothing to do with my title."

His lips twitched. "Not if they really knew you," he said.

"You flatter me," she said.

"Not because you're a princess," he said.

"Call me tomorrow."

"I will," he said.

Bridget returned to her table and tried to be her most charming self and at the same time not encouraging Robert Goodwin. It was challenging, but she was determined.

After the meal had been served, he turned to her. "I'm determined to dance with you."

"I'm not that good of a dancer," she assured him.

He laughed, his gaze dipping over her cleavage again. "I'm a good leader," he said and rose, extending his hand to her. "Let me surprise you."

Or not, she thought wishing with all her heart that he wouldn't surprise her. She didn't want to embarrass the man. She lifted her lips in a careful smile. "One dance," she said and stood.

They danced to a waltz, but he somehow managed to rub against her. She tried to back away, but he wrapped his hands around her waist like a vise, drawing him against her. Suddenly, she saw Ryder behind Robert Goodwin, his hand on his shoulder. Robert appeared surprised.

"Can I cut in?" Ryder asked.

Robert frowned. "I'm not—"

"Yes," Bridget said. "It's only proper."

Robert reluctantly released her and Ryder swept her into his arms.

"Thank goodness," she murmured.

He wrapped his arms around her and it felt entirely different than it had with Robert. She stared into his eyes and felt a shockwave roll through her. "When did you learn to dance?"

"A generous woman taught me during medical school," he said, drawing her closer, yet not too close.

Bridget felt a spike of envy but forced it aside. "She did an excellent job."

He chuckled. "It was all preparation," he said. "Everything we do is preparation for what waits for us in the future."

"I would have to be quite arrogant to think your preparation was for me," she said, feeling light-headed.

"You look beautiful tonight," he said, clearly changing the subject. "I hate having to share you with anyone else."

Her stomach dipped. "It's part of who I was born to be. Duty calls," she said.

"But what does Bridget want?" he challenged. "Meet me in the foyer in fifteen minutes."

"How?" she asked.

"You'll figure it out," he said.

Chapter Five

S*he would figure it out,* Bridget thought as she surreptitiously glanced at the diamond-encrusted watch that had belonged to her grandmother. Two minutes to go and she was supposed to be introduced to the crowd within the next moment.

"As we continue to introduce our honored guests, we'd like to present Her Highness, Princess Bridget Devereaux of the country of Chantaine."

Bridget stood and smiled and waved to the applauding crowd. She hadn't known she was a table head, but it wasn't unusual for event organizers to put her in the spotlight given the chance. Because of her title, she was a source of curiosity and interest.

Spotting Ryder leaning against the back wall as he pointed to his watch, she quickly squeezed her hand together and flashed her five fingers, indicating she needed more time. Then she sank into her seat.

Robert leaned toward her. "I was cheated out of my dance. We need to hit the floor again."

"I wish I could, but my ankle is hurting," she said.

Robert scowled. "Maybe because of the man who cut in on our dance."

She lifted her shoulders. "Perhaps it's the long day catching up with me."

"You're too generous. We could try a slow dance," he said in a low voice.

"Oh no, I couldn't hurt your feet that way," she said. "But I would like to freshen up. Please excuse me," she said and rose, wondering why she was going to such extremes to meet Ryder when she was supposed to be concentrating on making an appearance.

Her heart was slamming against her rib cage as she tried to take a sideways route through the tables along the perimeter of the room. With every step, part of her chanted *This is crazy—this is crazy.* But she kept on walking, so she must indeed be crazy. She stepped into the foyer and glanced around the area.

Something snagged her hand. She glanced over her shoulder and spotted Ryder as he pulled her with him down a hallway. "Where are we—"

"Trust me," he said and pulled her toward the first door they came upon. It was an empty dark room with a stack of chairs pushed against a wall.

"What are we doing?" she asked, breathlessly clinging to him.

"Hell if I know," he said, sliding his hands through her hair and tilting her head toward his. "I feel like a car with no brakes headed straight for you."

"So, we're both crazy," she said.

"Looks that way," he said and lowered his mouth to hers.

Her knees turned to water and she clung to him. His strength made her feel alive despite how tired she felt from her long day of travel. Shocked at his effect on her, she loved the sensation of his hard chest against her breasts. She wanted to feel his naked skin against hers. She growled, unable to get close enough.

He swore under his breath as his hands roamed over her waist and up to the sides of her breasts. "I can't get enough of you," he muttered and took her mouth in a deep kiss again.

She felt dizzy with a want and need she denied on a regular basis. It was as if she was suffering from a more delicious version of altitude sickness. His mouth against hers made her hotter with every stroke of his tongue. More than anything, she wanted to feel him against her.

"Ryder," she whispered, tugging at his tie and dropping her mouth to his neck.

He gave a groan of arousal. "Come home with me. Now," he said, squeezing her derriere with one hand and clasping her breast with the other.

Too tempted for words, she felt the tug and pull of duty and courtesy over her own needs. Bloody hell, why couldn't she just this once be selfish, irresponsible and rude? A sound of complete frustration bubbled from her throat. Because she just couldn't. She was in the States on official business from Chantaine and she'd been assigned to represent a cause important to her and her people.

"I can't," she finally managed. "It would just be

wrong and rude and it's not just about me. I'm sorry," she whispered.

"I don't know what it is about you, but you make me want to be more reckless than I've ever been in my life. More reckless than flying down Deadman's Hill on my bicycle with no hands when I was ten."

Bridget felt the same way, but she was holding on by the barest thread of self-restraint. Suddenly the door whooshed open and closed, sending her heart into her throat. Her head cleared enough to realize this situation could provide the press with an opportunity to paint her family in a bad light.

She held her breath, waiting for a voice, but none sounded.

"It's okay," he said as if he understood without her saying a word. "Whoever opened the door must have glanced inside and not spotted us. I'll leave first, then you wait a minute or two before you leave. I'll warn you if it looks like there's a crowd waiting for you."

She paused, then nodded slowly.

Ryder gave her shoulders a reassuring squeeze and kissed her quickly, then walked toward the door. Bridget stood frozen to the floor for several breaths and gave herself a quick shake. She moved to the door and listened, but the door was too thick. She couldn't hear anything. Counting to a hundred, she cracked open the door and peeked outside. No crowd. No photogs. Relief coursed through her and she stepped outside.

"Your Highness, I was worried about you," Robert said from behind her.

Her stomach muscles tightened and she quickly turned. "Robert, how kind of you."

"What were you doing in there?" he asked.

"My sense of direction is dismal," she said. "I went right when I should have turned left. Thank you for coming to my rescue. Now I can return to our table."

He slid his hand behind her waist and she automatically stiffened, but he seemed to ignore her response. "We can leave, if you like. I could take you to my condo...."

"Again, you're being kind, but we're here for an important cause."

"Afterward—"

"It's been a full day for me flying from Chicago. I appreciate your understanding that I'll be desperate to finally retire," she said. One of her advisers had instructed her that one should speak to another person as if they possessed good qualities...even if they didn't.

"Another time, then," Robert said, clearly disappointed.

Bridget gave a noncommittal smile, careful not to offer any false hope.

When Bridget didn't hear from Ryder for three days, she began to get peeved. Actually, she was peeved after day one. He'd behaved like he was starving for her and couldn't wait another moment, then didn't call. She considered calling him at least a dozen times, but her busy schedule aided her in her restraint.

On Tuesday, however, she was scheduled to meet with a preventative adult health specialist in preparation for a video she would be filming with the doctor as a public service announcement for Chantaine.

Afterward, she meandered down the hall past his

office. She noticed Ryder wasn't there, but his assistant was. Bridget gave in to temptation and stepped into the office. "Hello. I was wondering if Dr. McCall is in today."

The assistant sighed. "Dr. McCall is making rounds and seeing interns, but he may need to leave early for family reasons. May I take a message?"

"Not necessary," she demurred, but wondered what those family reasons were. "Are the twins okay?" she couldn't help asking.

The assistant nodded. "I think so. It's the nanny—" The phone rang. "Excuse me."

The nanny! The nanny she'd selected for Ryder and the boys had been as perfect as humanly possible. Perhaps more perfect. What could have possibly happened? Resisting the urge to grill the assistant about her, she forced herself to walk away. Her fingers itched to call him, but she didn't. It would be rude to interrupt his appointments with patients or the residents.

Bothered, bothered, bothered, she stalked through the hallway. The pediatric department head saw her and stopped in front of her, smiling. "Your Highness, what a pleasure to see you."

"Thank you, Doctor. How are you?" she said more than asked.

"Great. Would you like to get together for dinner?" he asked.

"I would, but I must confess my immediate schedule is quite demanding. Perhaps some other time," she said.

"I'll keep asking," he said and gave her a charming smile that didn't move her one iota.

Brooding, she walked down the hall and out of the hospital to the limo that awaited her. A text would be less intrusive, she decided, and sent a message. Two minutes later, she received a response. *Nanny had emergency appendectomy. Juggling with backup.*

WHY DIDN'T YOU CALL ME? she texted in return.

Her phone rang one moment later and she answered. "Hello."

"It's been crazy. I've even had to ask Marshall for help."

"Why didn't you ask me?" she demanded.

"You told me your schedule was picking up. I figured you wouldn't have time," he said.

True, she thought, but she was still bothered. "You still should have called me."

"You're a busy princess. What could you have done?" he asked.

Good question. She closed her eyes. "I could have rearranged my schedule so I could help you."

Silence followed. "You would do that?"

She bit her lip. "Yes."

"I didn't think of that."

"Clearly," she said.

He chuckled. "In that case, can you come over tomorrow afternoon? My part-time nanny needs a break."

"I'll confirm by five o'clock tonight," she said. "I have to make a few calls."

"Impressive," he said. "I bet your reschedules are going to be disappointed. Too bad," he said without a trace of sympathy.

She laughed. "I'll call you later," she said and they hung up and her heart felt ten times lighter.

The following afternoon, Bridget relieved the backup nanny while the twins were sleeping. From previous experience, she knew her moments of silence were numbered. She used the time to prepare bottles and snacks for the boys.

Sure enough, the first cry sounded. She raced upstairs and opened the door. Travis was sitting up in his crib wearing a frowny face.

"Hello, sweet boy," she whispered.

He paused mid-wail and stared at her wide-eyed.

"Hi," she whispered and smiled.

Travis smiled and lifted his fingers to his mouth.

Bridget changed his diaper. Seconds later, Tyler awakened and began to babble. Tyler was the happier baby. He was a bit more fearful, but when he woke up, he didn't start crying immediately.

Bridget wound Travis's mobile and turned her attention to Tyler. She took each baby downstairs ready to put them in their high chairs. Snacks, bottles, books, Baby Einstein and finally Ryder arrived carrying a bottle of wine.

"How's everybody?" he asked, his gaze skimming over her and the boys, then back to her. "Did they wear you out?"

"Not too much yet," she said. "It helps to have a plan."

He nodded. "With alternatives. I ordered Italian, not pizza. It should be delivered soon."

"Thank you," she said.

"I'm hoping to lure you into staying the night," he said.

"Ha, ha," she said. "The trouble with luring me after an afternoon with the twins is that I'll be comatose by nine o'clock at the latest. I talked to your part-time sitter and she told me Suzanne will be out for a few more days. Is that true?"

He nodded. "She had laparoscopic surgery, so her recovery should be much easier than if she'd had an open appendectomy."

"Then I think the next step is to get a list of your backup sitters and inform them of the situation and make a schedule for the children's care. So if you don't mind giving me your names and contact information, I can try to get it straight tomorrow."

He blinked at her in amazement. "You're deceptively incredible," he said. "You give this impression of being lighthearted and maybe a little superficial. Then you turn around and volunteer to take care of my boys, recruit doctors for your country and make countless appearances."

"Oooh, I like that. Deceptively incredible," she said, a bit embarrassed by his flattery. "Many of us are underestimated. It can be a hindrance and a benefit. I try to find the benefit."

Ryder leaned toward her, studying her face. "Have you always been underestimated?"

She considered his question for a moment, then nodded. "I think so. I'm number four out of six and female, so I think I got lost in the mix. I'm not sure my father ever really knew my name, and my mother was beginning to realize that her marriage to my father was not going to be a fairy tale."

"Why not?"

"You must swear to never repeat this," she said.

"I swear, although I'm not sure anyone I know would be interested," he said.

"True enough," she said. "My father was a total philanderer. Heaven knows, my mother tried. I mean, six children? She was a true soldier, though, and gave him two sons. Bless her."

"So what do you want for yourself?" he asked. "You don't want the kind of marriage your parents had."

"Who would?" she said and took a deep breath. "I haven't thought a lot about it. Whenever Stefan has brought up the idea of my marrying someone, I just start laughing and don't stop. Infuriates the blazes out of him," she said, and smiled.

"You didn't answer my question," he said.

His eyes felt as if they bored a hole through her brain, and Bridget realized one of the reasons she was drawn to Ryder was because she couldn't fool him. It was both a source of frustration and relief.

"I'm still figuring it out. For a long time, I've enjoyed the notion of being the eccentric princess who lives in Italy most of the year and always has an Italian boyfriend as her escort."

"Italian boyfriend," he echoed, clearly not pleased.

"You have to agree, it's the antithesis of my current life."

"And I suspect this life wouldn't include children," he continued with a frown.

Feeling defensive, she bit her lip. "Admit it. The life

you'd planned didn't include children…at least for a long while, did it?"

He hesitated.

"Be honest. I was," she said.

"No," he finally admitted. "But not because I was in Italy with an Italian girlfriend."

"No, you were planning to do something more important. A career in medicine. Perfectly noble and worthy, but it would be hard to make a child a priority when you have the kind of passion you do for your career. A child would be…inconvenient."

He took a deep breath. "We choose our careers for many reasons. I wanted to feel like I had the power to help, to cure, to make a difference. It was more important for me to feel as if I were accomplishing those goals than building a family life." He shrugged. "My family life sucked."

"There you go," she said in complete agreement. "My family life sucked, too. In fact, I wanted to get so far away from it that I wanted to move to a different country."

He chuckled. "So how is it that Princess Bridget is changing diapers and taking care of my twins?"

Bridget resisted the urge to squirm. "I won't lie. I once thought children were a lot of trouble and not for me, but then I got a couple of adorable nieces. I still thought I wouldn't want to deal with them for more than a couple hours at most with the nanny at hand to change diapers, of course." She bit her lip. "But it's just so different when they're looking at you with those big eyes, helpless and needing you…. And it would just feel so terribly wrong not to take care of them."

"And how do I fit into it?" he asked, dipping his head toward her.

"You are just an annoying distraction," she said in a mockingly dismissive whisper.

"Well, at least I'm distracting," he said and lowered his mouth to hers.

Bridget felt herself melt into the leather upholstery. She inhaled his masculine scent and went dizzy with want. He was the one thing she'd never had but always wanted and couldn't get enough of. How could that be? She'd been exposed to everything and every kind of person, hadn't she?

But Ryder was different.

She drew his tongue deeper into her mouth and slid her arms around his neck. Unable to stop herself, she wiggled against him and moaned. He groaned in approval, which jacked her up even more.

From some corner of her mind, she heard a sound.

"Eh."

Pushing it aside, she continued to kiss Ryder.

"Eh."

Bridget frowned, wondering....

"Wahhhhhhh."

She reluctantly tore her mouth from Ryder's. "The babies," she murmured breathlessly, glancing down at Travis as he tuned up. The baby had fallen on his side and he couldn't get back up.

"Yeah, I know," Ryder said. "I'm starting to understand the concept of unrequited l—"

"Longing," she finished for him because she couldn't deal with Ryder saying the four-letter L word. It wasn't possible.

"Bet there's a dirty diaper involved," Ryder muttered as he tilted Travis upright.

"Could be," she said and couldn't bring herself to offer to change it. She covered her laugh by clearing her throat. "I wouldn't want to deprive you of your fatherly duty."

He gave her a slow, sexy grin. "I'll just bet you wouldn't."

"It's an important bonding activity," she said, trying to remain serious, but a giggle escaped.

"Can't hold it against you too much," he said. "You've been here all afternoon."

Bridget rose to try to collect herself. Her emotions were all over the place. Walking to the downstairs powder room, she closed the door behind her and splashed water against her cheeks and throat. Sanity, she desperately needed sanity.

The doorbell rang and she returned as Ryder tossed the diaper into the trash before he answered the door. He paid the delivery man and turned around, and Bridget felt her heart dip once, twice, three times…. Adrenaline rushed through her, and she tried to remember a charming, gorgeous Italian man who had affected her this way. When had any man affected her this way?

Oh, heavens, she needed to get away from him. She felt like that superhero. What was his name? Superman. And Ryder was that substance guaranteed to weaken him. What was it? Started with a K…

"Smells good. Hope you like lasagna," Ryder said.

"I can't stay," she said.

"What?" he asked, his brow furrowing.

"I can't stay. I have work to do," she said.

"What work?" he asked.

"Rescheduling my meetings and appearances. I also need to take care of the childcare arrangements for the twins."

He walked slowly toward her, his gaze holding hers. She felt her stomach tumble with each of his steps. "You're not leaving because you have work to do, are you?"

She lifted her chin. "I'm a royal. I always have work to do."

He cupped her chin with his hand. "But the reason you're leaving is not because of work, is it?"

Her breath hitched in her throat.

"You're a chicken, aren't you?" he said. "Princess Cluck Cluck."

"That was rude," she said.

"Cluck, cluck," he said and pressed his mouth against hers.

After making the schedule for the twins' care, Bridget paid her sister an overdue visit. Valentina had threatened to personally drag her away from Dallas if Bridget didn't come to the ranch. Her sister burst down the steps to the porch as Bridget's limo pulled into the drive.

"Thank goodness you're finally here," Tina said.

Bridget laughed as she embraced her sister. "You act like I've been gone for years."

"I thought you would be spending far more time here, but you've been appearing at events, traveling to Chicago. And what's this about you helping that physician with his twin babies? Haven't you helped him enough?"

"It's complicated," Bridget said. "He's had some childcare issues. I think they're mostly resolved now."

"Well, good. I think you've helped him quite enough. Now you can spend some time with me," Tina said as she led Bridget into the house. "I have wonderful plans for us. Two aestheticians are coming to the ranch tomorrow to give massages and facials then we spend the afternoon at the lake."

"Lake?" Bridget echoed. All she'd seen was dry land.

"It's wonderful," Tina reassured her. "The summer heat and humidity can get unbearable here. We have a pond with a swing, but we're going to the lake because Zach got a new boat. Zach and one of his friends will be joining us tomorrow afternoon. Then we'll have baby back ribs for dinner."

Bridget's antennae went up at the mention of Zach's friend. "You're not trying to set me up, are you?"

"Of course not. I just thought you'd enjoy some no-pressure male companionship. Troy is just a nice guy. He also happens to be good-looking and eligible. And if you two should hit it off, then you could live close to me and—" Tina paused and a guilty expression crossed her face. "Okay, it's a little bit of a setup. But not too much," she said quickly. "Troy and Zach are business associates, so we'll have to drag them away from talk about the economy."

Bridget's mind automatically turned to Ryder. There was no reason for her to feel even vaguely committed to him. Her stomach tightened. What did that mean? she wondered. "I'm not really looking right now," Bridget said.

"I know," Tina said. "As soon as you take care of the

doctor project, you're off to Italy and part of that will include flirtations with any Italian man who grabs your fancy. But if someone here grabs your fancy…"

"Tina," Bridget said in a warning voice.

"I hear you," Tina said. "Let's focus on your amazing niece."

"Sounds good to me. I've missed the little sweetheart," Bridget said as they walked into the kitchen.

"Missed her, but not me!" Tina said.

Bridget laughed. "I adore you. Why are you giving me such a hard time?"

Tina lifted her hand to Bridget's face and looked deep into her gaze. "I don't know. I worry about you. I wonder what's going on inside you. You smile, you laugh, but there's a darkness in your eyes."

Bridget's heart dipped at her sister's sensitivity, then she deadpanned. "Maybe it's my new eyeliner."

Tina rolled her eyes. "You're insufferable. I always said that about Stefan, but you're the same, just in a different way."

"I believe I've just been insulted," Bridget said.

"You'll get over it. Hildie made margaritas for us and she always makes doubles."

Chapter Six

Bridget's morning massage coupled with one of Hildie's margaritas had turned her bones to butter. By the time she joined Tina, Zach and Troy on the boat, she was so relaxed that she could have gone to sleep for a good two hours. For politeness' sake, she tried to stay awake, although she kept her dark sunglasses firmly in place to hide her drooping eyelids.

Troy Palmer was a lovely Texas gentleman, a bit bulkier than Ryder. Of course Ryder was so busy he rarely took time to eat. A server offered shrimp and lobster while they lounged on the boat.

"Nice ride," Troy said to Zach.

Zach smiled as Tina leaned against his chest. "My wife thought I was crazy. She said I would be too busy."

"Time will tell," Tina said. "But if this makes you take a few more breaks, then I'm happy."

"You're not neglecting my sister, are you?" Bridget asked as she sipped a bottle of icy cold water.

Zach lifted a dark eyebrow. "There's a fine line between being the companion and keeper of a princess."

"I believe that's what you Americans call baloney. You work because you must. It's the kind of man you are. I love you for it," Tina said. "But I also love the time we have together."

Zach's face softened. "I love you, too, sweetheart."

Bridget cleared her throat. "We're delighted that you love each other," Bridget said. "But I'm going to have to dive overboard if we don't change the subject."

Tina giggled. "As you wish. Troy, tell us about your latest trip to Italy."

"Italy?" Bridget echoed.

"I thought that might perk you up," Tina said.

Troy shrugged his shoulders. "I go three or four times a year. Business, but I usually try to work in a trip to Florence."

"Oh, Florence," Bridget said longingly. "One of my favorite places in the world."

Troy nodded. "Yeah, I also like to slip down to Capri every now and then…"

Bridget's cell phone vibrated in the pocket of her cover-up draped over the side of her chair. She tried to ignore it, but wondered if Ryder was calling her. Dividing her attention between Troy's discussion about Italy and thoughts of Ryder, she nodded even though she wasn't hanging onto his every word. Her phone vibrated again and she was finding it difficult to concentrate.

She grabbed her cover-up and stood. "Please excuse me. I need to powder my nose."

"To the right and downstairs," Zach said. "And it's small," he warned.

"No problem," she said cheerfully and walked around the corner. She lifted her phone to listen to her messages. As she listened, her heart sank. Tomorrow's sitter was canceling. She was calling Bridget because Ryder was in surgery and unreachable.

Pacing at the other end of the boat, she tried the other backup sitters and came up empty. Reluctantly, she called Marshall who answered immediately.

"Marshall," he said. "'Sup?"

"Hello, Marshall," she said. "This is Bridget Devereaux."

"The princess," he said. Ryder had told her that Marshall had performed a web search and learned who she was. "Princess calling me. That's cool."

"Yes," she said, moving toward the other end of the boat. "There's some difficulty with sitting arrangements for Ryder's boys tomorrow morning. I was hoping you could help me with a solution."

"Tomorrow morning," he said. "Whoa, that's a busy day for me."

"Yes, I'm so sorry. I would normally try to fill in, but I'm out of town at the moment," she said.

"I might have a friend—"

"No," she said. "As you know, Ryder is very particular about his backup sitters. He won't leave the twins with just anyone."

"True," Marshall said. "Although I'm last on the list." Silence followed.

"I'm last on the list, aren't I?" Marshall asked.

"Well, you're an entrepreneur," she managed. "Ryder

knows you're a busy man with many demands on your time."

"Yeah," Marshall said. "How much time does he need?"

"Five hours," she said, wincing as she said it.

Marshall whistled. "That's gonna be tough."

"Let me see what I can do," she said. "I'll make some more calls."

"If you can have someone cover things in the early morning, I could probably come in around ten."

"Thank you so much. I'll do my very best," she said.

"Bridget," Tina said from behind her.

"Bloody hell," she muttered.

Marshall chuckled.

"To whom are you speaking?" Tina demanded.

"A friend," Bridget said. "Forgive me, Marshall. My sister is after me."

"Good luck. Keep me posted," he said.

"Yes, I will," she said and clicked off the phone. She turned to face her sister with a smile. "I'm just working out the timing of an appearance."

"Which appearance is that?" Tina asked.

"In Dallas," Bridget said. "I must say I do love Zach's new toy. I think it will be a fabulous way for the two of you to relax."

"Exactly which appearance in Dallas?" Tina said, studying her with narrowed eyes.

"Stop being so nosy," Bridget said.

Tina narrowed her eyes further. "This is about that doctor with the twins, isn't it?"

"His sitter for tomorrow has cancelled so we have to find another."

"We?"

Bridget sighed. "If you met him, you'd understand. He performs surgery, advises residents and he's an instant father."

"Perhaps he should take some time off to be with his new children," Tina muttered.

"It's not that easy. His mentor has Alzheimer's and he's trying to fill his position unofficially."

Tina studied her. "You're not falling for him, are you?"

Bridget gave a hearty laugh at the same time she fought the terror in her soul. "Of course not. You know I prefer Italian men."

Tina paused, then nodded. "True, and although you love your nieces, you've always said you couldn't imagine having children before you were thirty."

"Exactly," she said, though she felt a strange twinge.

"Hmm," Tina said, still studying her. "Is this doctor good-looking?"

Bridget shrugged. Yes, Ryder was very good-looking, but that wasn't why she found him so compelling. Giving herself a mental eye roll, she knew Tina wouldn't understand. "He's fine," she said. "But he's not Italian."

Tina giggled and put her arm around Bridget. "Now that's our Bridget. That's the kind of answer I would expect from you. Come back and relax with us."

Bridget smiled, but part of her felt uncomfortable. She knew what Tina was saying, that Bridget wasn't a particularly deep person. The truth was she'd never wanted to be deep. If she thought too deeply, she suspected she could become depressed. After all, she'd been a fairly average child, not at all spectacular. She hadn't flunked out in school, but she hadn't excelled at anything either. Except at being cheerful. Or pretending to be cheerful.

"I'll be there in just a moment. I need to make a few calls first."

"Very well, but don't take too long. Troy may not be Italian, but he's very good-looking and spends a fair amount of time in Italy."

"Excellent point," Bridget said, although she felt not the faintest flicker of interest in the man. "I'll be there shortly."

Several moments later, Bridget used all her charm to get the part-time sitter to fill in for the morning. Relieved, she called Marshall to inform him of the change.

"Hey, did you hear from Ryder?" he asked before she could get a word in edgewise.

"No. Should I have?" she asked, confused. "I thought he was in surgery."

"He's apparently out. He just called to tell me Dr. Walters passed away this morning," Marshall said.

Bridget's heart sank. "Oh no."

"Yeah. He's taking it hard. He hadn't seen Dr. Walters in a while and he'd been planning to try to visit him later this week." Marshall sighed. "Dr. Walters was the closest thing to a father Ryder had."

Bridget felt so helpless. "Is there something I can do?"

"Not really," Marshall said. "The twins will keep him busy tonight and that's for the best. The next few days are gonna be tough, though."

She saw her sister walking toward her and felt conflicted. "Thank you for telling me."

"No problem. Thanks for taking care of the childcare for tomorrow morning. Bye for now."

"Goodbye," she said, but he had already disconnected.

"You look upset," Tina said.

"I am."

After 9:30 p.m., Ryder prowled his den with a heavy heart. His mentor was gone. Although Dr. Walters had been mentally gone for a while now, the finality of the man's physical death hit Ryder harder than he'd expected. Maybe it was because he'd lost his brother so recently, too.

Ryder felt completely and totally alone. Sure, he had the twins and his profession, but two of the most important people in the world to him were gone and never coming back. He wondered what it meant that aside from his longtime friend Marshall, he had no other meaningful relationships. Was he such a workaholic that he'd totally isolated himself?

A knock sounded on his door, surprising him. Probably Marshall, he thought and opened the door. To Bridget. His heart turned over.

"Hi," she said, her gaze searching his. She bit her lip. "I know it's late and I don't want to impose—"

He snagged her arm and pulled her inside. "How did you know?"

"Marshall," she said, then shot him a chiding glance. "I would have preferred to hear it from you."

"I thought about it," he said, raking his hand through his hair. "But you've done enough helping with the babies."

"I thought perhaps that you and I were about more

than the babies, but maybe I was wrong," she said, looking away.

His heart slamming against his rib cage, he cupped her chin and swiveled it toward him. "You were right. You know you were."

"Is it just sex? Are you just totally deprived?" she asked in an earnest voice.

He swallowed a chuckle. "I wish."

Her eyes darkened with emotion and she stepped closer. She moved against him and slid her arms upward around the back of his neck. She pulled his face toward hers and he couldn't remember feeling this alive. Ever.

His lips brushed hers and he tried to hold on to his self-control, but it was tough. She slid her moist lips from side to side and he couldn't stand it any longer. He devoured her with his mouth, tasting her, taking her. Seconds later, he realized he might not ever get enough, but damn, he would give it his best shot.

He slid his fingers through her hair and slid his tongue deeper into her mouth. She suckled it and wriggled against him. Her response made him so hard that he wasn't sure he could stand it. His body was on full tilt in the arousal zone.

He took a quick breath and forced himself to draw back. "I'm not sure I can pull back after this," he said, sliding his hands down over her waist and hips. "If you're going to say no, do it now."

Silence hung between them for heart-stopping seconds.

He sucked in another breath. "Bridget—"

"Yes," she whispered. "Yes."

Everything in front of him turned black and white

at the same time. He drew her against him and ran his hands up to her breasts and her hair, then back down again. He wanted to touch every inch of her.

She felt like oxygen to him, like life after he'd been in a tomb. He couldn't get enough of her. He savored the taste and feel of her. Tugging at her blouse, he pushed it aside and slid his hands over her shoulders and lower to the tops of her breasts.

She gave a soft gasp that twisted his gut.

"Okay?" he asked, dipping his thumbs over her nipples.

She gasped again. "Yesssss."

He unfastened her bra and filled his hands with her breasts.

Ryder groaned. Bridget moaned.

"So sexy," he muttered.

She pulled at his shirt and seconds later, her breasts brushed his chest. Ryder groaned again.

The fire inside him exploded and he pushed aside the rest of her clothes and his. He tasted her breasts and slid his mouth lower to her belly and lower still, drawing more gasps and moans from her delicious mouth. Then he thought about contraception. Swearing under his breath, he pulled back for a second. "Give me a few seconds," he said. "You'll thank me later."

He raced upstairs to grab condoms and returned downstairs.

"What?" she asked.

"Trust me," he said and took her mouth again. He slid his hand between her legs and found her wet and wanting.

Unable to hold back one moment longer, he pushed

her legs apart and sank inside her. Bridget clung to him as he pumped inside her. She arched against him, drawing him deep.

He tried to hold out, but she felt so good. Plunging inside her one last time, he felt his climax roar through him. Alive, he felt more alive than he'd felt for as long as he could remember…. "Bridget," he muttered.

Her breath mingled with his and he could sense that she hadn't gone over the top. He was determined to take her there. Sliding his hand between them, he found her sweet spot and began to stroke.

Her breath hitched. The sound was gratifying and arousing. A couple moments later, she stiffened beneath him. He began to thrust again and she came in fits and starts, sending him over the edge.

He couldn't believe his response to her. Twice in such a short time? He wasn't an eighteen-year-old. "Come to bed with me."

"Yes," she said. "If I can make my legs move enough to walk upstairs."

He chuckled and knew the sound was rough. Everything about him felt sated, yet aroused and rough. "I'll help."

"Thank goodness," she said.

He helped her to her feet, but when they arrived at the bottom of the steps, he swept her into his arms and carried her up the stairs.

"Oh, help," she said. "I hope I don't give you a hernia."

"If you do, it'll be worth it," he said.

She swatted at him. "You're supposed to say I'm as light as a feather even though I may weigh half a ton."